FOREVERLAND

FOREVERLAND

NICOLE C. KEAR

{Imprint}
MAKE YOUR MARK

New York

[Imprint]
MAKE YOUR MARK

A part of Macmillan Publishing Group, LLC
120 Broadway, New York, NY 10271

FOREVERLAND. Copyright © 2020 by Nicole C. Kear. All rights reserved.
Printed in the United States of America by
LSC Communications, Harrisonburg, Virginia.

Library of Congress Cataloging-in-Publication Data is available.

ISBN 978-1-250-21983-1 (hardcover) / ISBN 978-1-250-21984-8 (ebook)

Our books may be purchased in bulk for promotional, educational, or business use. Please contact your local bookseller or the Macmillan Corporate and Premium Sales Department at (800) 221-7945 ext. 5442 or by email at MacmillanSpecialMarkets@macmillan.com.

Book design by Elynn Cohen

Imprint logo designed by Amanda Spielman

First edition, 2020

1   3   5   7   9   10   8   6   4   2

mackids.com

For my **G**irls, believers

In magic. And for my Boy Wonder, who

Opened these gates.

For a while, I'm dropping

Off the

Radar.

Everything's so

Very screwed up, I can't

Even stand the thought of home.

Running away is a

Lousy idea but it's

Also my only idea. And

Nowhere else will

Do.

CHAPTER 1

Fun fact: I am running away. To live in an amusement park.

Related fact: I am not a runaway kind of person. Unless you're talking about running away from a fight, or from awkward eye contact or something. Then, yes, totally, I'm your girl.

But if you made everyone in my sixth-grade class vote for "Least Likely to Run Away to Live in an Amusement Park," they'd definitely pick me. If they could remember my name.

So it's kind of unbelievable that I am here, standing directly in front of the Foreverland gates, in the middle of a Wednesday in the middle of the summer, when everyone thinks I'm at computer camp back in the city.

Life is full of surprises.

People say that like it's a good thing, but honestly, the surprises are usually bad ones. At best, it's 50/50. Of course, I'm a glass-half-empty kind of person—at least that's what my mom tells me. So I might be wrong. But, just as an example, the suitcase

I found this morning by the door—*that* was a surprise. And not the party-hat kind, that's for sure.

This, here, my running away—I haven't decided yet if it's a good surprise or a bad one. Because I haven't decided yet whether I'm really doing this. Yes, I took the Metro-North from Grand Central for an hour and a half, then the Foreverland shuttle bus to get here, but I haven't really done anything that wrong yet. I haven't done anything I can't undo.

I crane my neck up to look at the FOREVERLAND sign hanging in the middle of the gate. Underneath, in smaller letters, it says: WHERE MAGIC NEVER ENDS! I look past the gate and see the sweep of coasters curving like mysterious symbols in the sky. I breathe in the tangy, plasticky smell of cotton candy from a nearby stand. If the color pink had a scent, this would be it. I hear the joyful shrieks of people riding high, cutting through clouds. It looks and smells and sounds like freedom and fun and, yes, maybe even magic. And it can all be mine . . . if I step inside.

Chances are, I'll get caught right away. I mean, there are definitely people who could pull this thing off—fast-thinking, slick-talking criminal masterminds—but I am not one of those people. I panic when I order from the "12 and under" menu, even though I *am* twelve, because it feels like I'm just cutting it a little too close. This will never, *never* work.

I could just spin around, retrace my steps, take the train to the city, and be back before my parents get home.

Home.

Home.

I can think of about a hundred reasons why I shouldn't take another step forward.

But I do.

I take another step. I walk through the gates. Right into Foreverland.

CHAPTER 2

I head to the ticket booth, weaving around a swarm of little kids in mustard-yellow Camp Barrie T-shirts. The ticket line is really long. I knew the park would be busy, since it's the middle of the day, but the park is even more packed than I'd expected. Which is great. Perfect, actually.

The bigger the crowd, the easier it is to get lost in.

And since getting lost in the crowd is one of my specialties, I'm all set.

Fun fact: I'm a wallflower.

Actually, I'm more like wall paint. I'm pretty sure flowered wallpaper gets more attention than I do.

I guess it's because I'm quiet or maybe I have one of those faces that looks like a lot of other faces. Either way, lots of people forget they've met me. I know this is a thing that happens once in a while to people, but it happens all the time to me. It's hard not to be insulted. Nobody wants to be invisible.

Except for superheroes, as my ex-best friend Priya would point out when I complained about this. Spies, too.

"You're looking at this all wrong," she'd say. "Think of the perks of blending in."

This, right here, is one of those perks. When you're running away to live in an amusement park, it comes in handy to have the kind of face people instantly forget.

I'm happy the park is crowded, but I'm not thrilled that the ticket line is so long. The longer I wait, the more nervous I get. It's boiling hot out and I'm sweating up a storm, but I've got cold feet, all right—feet so cold they're turning icy. My heart's racing and my stomach gets that familiar churning feeling.

I do the one thing that I know will definitely calm me down.

I write an acrostic poem.

I take my brand-new notebook out of my backpack, uncap a Flair pen, and scribble:

A
C
R
O
S
T
I
C

Then I fill it in:

A kind of weird way to

Calm down, but weird is

Relative. It's not nearly as

Odd as that

Sixteen-year-old I read about who

Turns her fingernail clippings

Into sculptures, as a way to

Chill.

Acrostics are my superpower. The only word I can't immediately turn into an acrostic is my name. It's my acrostic Kryptonite—it just makes my mind go blank. I tried to write one for my name this morning on the train. On the very first page of my new notebook, I wrote:

M

A

R

G

A

R

E

T

Just the bare skeleton of the acrostic. No meat on it. And it stayed that way. I couldn't fill it in.

I inch forward in the line. The closer I get to the ticket window, the more my heart speeds up. I scribble another acrostic:

Remember that the trick to

Effective

Lying is to say as little

As possible. Nothing

Xcept for what's necessary.

Okay, the last line is cheating a little, but *X*s are impossible to work with in an acrostic . . . I mean, there's *x-ray*, *xylophone*, and . . . I'm out.

Then it's my turn. I slip my notebook into my backpack, take out my money, and walk up to a ticket window. A grandma-type lady with short gray hair is asking me, "How many tickets?"

"One," I croak. "Youth. Ummm, ticket?"

Ticket Lady is wearing these red reading glasses attached to a beaded chain around her neck, and now she's peering at me over the tops of these glasses.

"How old are you?" Ticket Lady asks.

My heart is thundering in my chest and my palms are so clammy, my money's getting damp. I try to calm down by taking a deep breath, but I just end up making a gasp-y sound, like a person being strangled.

"Twelve?"

Here's the thing: I'm not even lying. But I'm short for my age, so I know Ticket Lady will think I'm lying. And that's enough to make me short-circuit.

Some people are calm under pressure. I'm calamitous under pressure.

Now Ticket Lady has taken her fingers off her keyboard, and she's leaning over her counter to look at me, which is definitely a bad, bad sign.

Please don't ask where my parents are, I think. *Please don't ask—*

"Where are your parents?" Ticket Lady asks.

Fun fact: I am a terrible liar. The worst. Pinocchio is smoother than I am.

My heart is pounding so loudly, I worry that she can hear it. She knows; I'm sure of it. She knows I'm here alone, and she probably knows it's because I'm running away, and in about five seconds she is going to call the police.

"My parents? They're, um, coming?" I say. "In a few minutes?" All my answers come out like questions.

This happens to me all the time, and it drives my mom nuts. She's always lecturing me: "When you make your voice go up, like this? It doesn't command respect? You see what I'm saying?"

I do now. I see exactly what she's saying because Ticket Lady, who is officially suspicious, is asking me, "So you're unaccompanied?"

"No!" I say, way too loudly. "My parents are here, it's just—I, um, I couldn't wait to come in, and my toddler—I mean, my *sister*, who is a toddler— she had an accident . . . a, uh, urination accident? So they went back to the—to our car? Which is in the lot. The *parking* lot."

It's like my mouth has been hijacked. I have zero control over the words coming out of it. It's a cruel twist of fate that when I should talk, I clam up completely, but when I need to be quiet, I'm Little Miss Chatterbox.

Ticket Lady is looking at me like she's trying to decide what to do. Now, I think, might be a good time to give her money.

I put forty-seven dollars in sweaty, crumpled bills on the counter and push them through the slot in the window.

Ticket Lady frowns, then looks behind me at the long line, which I am holding up. After a few seconds, she pulls my money through the window and stabs at a few keys on her keyboard, and then a tiny printer starts sputtering. My ticket.

I'm not the beaming type, but I beam.

"Have a magical day," she says. Her lips are pursed tight, like she is still really skeptical, so I don't think she genuinely wants me to have a magical day, but that's okay. I'll take it.

"Thanks!" I say. "You too!"

I walk over to the turnstiles, where a bored-looking teenager with hair down to his shoulders takes my ticket. He inserts it into the ticket-eating machine, which gobbles it up, and then the light on the turnstile turns green.

"Have a magical day," he mumbles in a monotone.

And just like that, I'm in. I am in Foreverland. And it's exactly how I remember it.

CHAPTER 3

"Souvenir photo?"

A woman in a Foreverland staff T-shirt with a huge camera hanging off her neck waves me over to a cheesy photo backdrop. It's a cloudless blue sky with mountains and lagoons and a white castle in the distance. On the top of the backdrop, the words *Where magic never ends!* are written in curly golden script.

I shake my head. I don't want to take a photo. But I stand looking at the backdrop, which I recognize. It's exactly the same as it was two summers ago, when I last came to Foreverland. Just to be sure, I slide my backpack off, unzip the front compartment, and pull out the photo I stashed there this morning. The picture that jump-started this whole idea.

In the photo is the same fairy-tale landscape, and in the middle of it is my family. Or the collection of people formerly known as my family. I don't know what to call us now.

We're all standing in a line. Mom's on the end, wearing a black skirt, a white embroidered shirt with fluttery sleeves, and big black sunglasses. That's her idea of casual. The woman does not own a single T-shirt or pair of sweatpants.

Next to her is my sister, Gwen, who's three years older than me. She looks just like Mom—same shoulder-length blonde hair, same brown eyes. Gwen's wearing a swim-team T-shirt and a pair of those athletic shorts that are ultra-everything: ultra-fast-dry and ultra-lightweight and ultra-expensive.

Next to Gwen is Dad, in his wrinkled Roosevelt College T-shirt and a pair of plaid shorts, with a black ink splotch near one pocket. He looks every bit like the head-in-the-clouds professor he is. He's sort of squinting behind his rectangular eyeglasses, and he's smiling his trademark toothy grin.

Next to Dad is me.

I'm wearing Gwen's hand-me-downs, like I always do, because they're in "excellent condition." They make me feel like I'm in a costume, but whatever. The T-shirt I'm wearing has a cartoon bumblebee on it, surrounded by the words BEE YOURSELF! You just don't get more ironic than that.

My hair is brownish, and longish, and straight-ish. It's in a low ponytail, the exact same kind of ponytail I have my hair in right now.

Mom's got her arm around Gwen, and Gwen's got her arm around Dad, and Dad's got his arm around me. We are pressing close together, so close that our bodies make a big block, a unit. If you looked at us from far away, we wouldn't look like four separate things. We'd look like one thing. We were, back then. We were a family.

This morning, when I found the photo, forgotten on the floor by the suitcase, all I wanted to do was jump into the picture. I didn't have a time machine, obviously. But I did have money for a train ticket.

And now I'm there. Here. Now I'm in Foreverland. I'm staring at the exact spot we stood two years ago.

All around me, fathers and mothers and brothers and sisters are veering off to Vertigo Vortex and Tsunami Falls and the Catapult and the Shooting Star, rushing to get there first so they won't have to wait so long. So they can cram more fun into their day. They only have one day, and they have to make the most of it.

Not me. I have all day and all night, too. When this place closes at ten, I'll be closed up inside it. Tomorrow when I wake, I can start all over again.

I grab a park map from the map kiosk. Then I stand under a tree to escape the brutal sun, and unfold it.

Foreverland has four sections: Sky City, Waterworld, Tot Town, and Magic Mile. Sky City has all the big roller coasters, Waterworld has all the—duh—water rides, Tot Town is the kiddie section, and Magic Mile—well, that has the miscellaneous stuff that doesn't fit in any of the other sections.

Foreverland isn't a theme park like Disneyland or whatever—it's smaller and a lot less famous. There are a few rides that are pretty well-known, like the Shooting Star, but there are definitely newer, nicer amusement parks closer to the city. The reason my family always came here was that Dad used to come when he was a kid, and he's got a soft spot for it.

So Foreverland doesn't have a theme really, except for the whole magic thing. There's signature "Magic Burgers" and "Magic Cones" and "Magic Hour." *Magic* is printed on basically every surface in the park.

I'm looking at the map, trying to decide what to ride first. I've been here so many times with my family—every summer for practically my whole life—and we have a strict routine developed by my control freak mom. We would come first thing in the morning, when the park opened, and we'd head straight to Sky City to get on the most popular rides before the park got too crowded. I never liked this plan.

Fun fact: I hate roller coasters.

Okay, I don't *hate* them. I'm not opposed to their existence. I just don't want to be on one, ever. They terrify me.

Is it ironic that I'm terrified of roller coasters but have run away to live in an amusement park?

Why, yes, it is.

Is it surprising?

Nope. Not at all.

I'm terrified of too many things to count. It'd be easier to make a list of the things I'm *not* terrified of.

I'm the only one in my family who doesn't like roller coasters. The rest of them are coaster-crazy. So we'd always beeline to the Shooting Star and the Catapult, where they'd get in line, and I'd wait on a nearby bench with a book.

"Honey. *Honey*," my mom would say, with her perfectly plucked eyebrows all raised, "are you really going to just sit there while we *all* ride? You're not even going to *try*?"

I'd really wanted to shoot back, "Are you really *all* going to ride while I sit here? You're not even going to *try* to consider what I want?"

But I'd never say that. I'd just shrug and open my book. And my mom would sigh and look so incredibly disappointed in me.

One summer, my parents got into a fight about it. They thought they were out of earshot, but they weren't. I'm lucky that way.

"Would you just leave her alone, Mary?" my dad said. "She's happy reading. Don't you get that?"

"She's not *happy* reading," my mom said. "She's *comfortable* reading. You never push her, which is exactly why she is the way she is."

I waited for my dad to ask, "And what way is that exactly?"

Because I wanted to know myself. But he didn't

ask—either because he knew what she meant already or because he was too fed up to keep talking.

Instead, Gwen chimed in. "Whatever, Mom, she's fine. Don't feel bad. It's an *amusement* park. The whole point is to go on the roller coasters, not to, like, ride the merry-go-round ten times."

Which made sense.

But it doesn't make sense now. Now it's my Foreverland, my way. And riding the merry-go-round ten times is exactly what I am going to do. Maybe I'll ride it *twenty* times. Who's going to stop me?

I walk toward the center of the park, to the Grand Carousel.

It's hot today. Blistering hot. Fry-an-egg-on-the-sidewalk hot. After about two minutes in the sun, I can feel my pale skin getting toasted like a marshmallow. So I stop under a tree to re-apply sunscreen. It's been a few hours since I put some on, while I was on the train.

I always carry sunscreen with me, ever since my fifth-grade science teacher taught a unit on climate change and I got terrified of skin cancer. Even Priya, who never worries about anything, started wearing sunscreen. I mean, what did Ms. McNally *think* would happen, showing us pictures of melanomas?

I sit on a bench overlooking Pirate's Cove and rub sunscreen carefully all over my arms, including the underside. I watch the boats sail by. Pirate's Cove is one of the oldest rides in the park and very low-key. There are these big pirate ships with benches along the sides, and you just slowly sail down the fake river and look out at the animatronic pirates doing pirate-y things — sword fighting, unrolling maps, singing sea chanteys.

As I watch the ships sail by, I notice something weird. There's a boy standing up at the front of one of the ships. I forget what you call that part — the fore? The aft? The helm?

He looks around my age, with wavy black hair and tanned skin, like he's been in the sun a lot. He has one foot up on the bench in front of him and his hands on his hips. But that's not even the weirdest part. The weirdest part is that he's looking right at me.

For a second, I think I'm imagining it. Then I think he's probably looking at somebody who's standing right behind me. That's happened to me before, and I made the mistake of saying, "Hi!" and then the other person said, "Umm, sorry, actually, I wasn't talking to you," and it was, oh, you know, excruciating.

So this time, I look behind me. There is nobody there. I turn back, and now the boy isn't just looking at me; he's *waving* at me.

Which makes zero sense. Zero.

I figure I have two options:

1. Ignore him. Which is pretty rude.
2. Wave back. And when he finds out I'm not who he thinks I am, die of humiliation.

So basically, all the choices are awkward, and I don't know what to do.

Which is exactly how I feel 100 percent of the time around most people.

I go with the first option. Rude is better than humiliated.

I slide the tube of sunscreen into my backpack and take off in the direction of the carousel.

Time to get merry and go round.

CHAPTER 4

I hear the carousel before I see it because the music is super loud. It's not that prerecorded stuff—it's actually being played on a band organ in the middle of the carousel.

A hundred years ago, every carousel had a band organ to make music, but now it's really rare to find a band organ that still works, which is why this carousel is so special and my favorite.

I tried to explain this to Gwen the last time we came to the park, two years ago.

"You lost me at 'band organ,'" Gwen said. "And if you lost me, seriously, you'll lose everyone."

"Oh, come on, now." Dad swooped to my rescue. "Band organs are very cool."

This came as no surprise, since he was the one who taught me about them.

"Imagine a supersized music box," he went on. "That's what we're talking about."

Gwen shook her head. "Nope. Even less interesting now."

I shoved Gwen and grinned at Dad, with an us-against-the-world kind of smile.

"It's interesting to *me*," I said.

Which is true, for better or worse.

Fun fact: I love music boxes.

Like, *love* love. So much that on the first day of sixth grade, when we were doing icebreakers in homeroom and my teacher asked us, "What's the one thing you'd take with you to live on a deserted island?" I said, "A music box."

Actually, I wish I'd only said "a music box." What I actually said was:

"Ummm, my collection of vintage music boxes . . . which, actually, I guess that's more than one thing—so then I'd take, just, um, my favorite one, which plays 'Over the Rainbow'—it's got this glass case so you can see the parts that make the music? Have you ever . . . It's like this metal sheet that rolls and hits these, um, nubs?"

Nubs. I used the word *nubs*. Could there possibly be a weirder word to use in the first five minutes of the first day of middle school?

I broke the ice, all right. I broke the thin ice of my social life, and I fell right through into freezing waters, and I died of hypothermia.

Fun fact: In middle school, you should just be yourself—but only if that self is like everyone else. Otherwise, be someone different.

Priya figured this out pretty quickly. It took me most of sixth grade to realize it, and by then, it was too late. My friendless fate was sealed.

Now, though, I can geek out as much as I want to about music boxes and band organs. So I follow the super-loud music until I see the bright blue roof that covers the carousel and the glint of all the golden poles. There's hardly any line—there never is, which is yet another reason it's my go-to ride.

I stand at the ride entrance behind a bunch of little kids, and while I wait, I check out the band organ in the center of the carousel. You can only see a part of it: the organ pipes, and on either side, two big drums. The rest of it is hidden behind these mirrored walls that make up a little hexagon-shaped room in the center of the merry-go-round.

I watch as the carousel slowly comes to a stop. The ride operator, a redheaded teenager with a face full of pimples, walks over to the little hexagon-shaped room in the middle of the carousel and pulls open a door. He disappears for a few seconds, and then comes out again with a Foreverland baseball cap on his head. He must be worried about skin cancer, too. Then he opens the gate to the ride. I head straight to the crocodile.

The Grand Carousel is not a horses-only merry-go-round. It's multispecies. Even mythical beasts are included, like centaurs and dragons. The unicorn is, hands down, the crowd favorite, but I prefer the croc.

Croc is not for everyone—or, really, anyone except for me. I've never seen anyone else ride him.

His eyes are rolled upward and his position is mid-thrash, like he's ripping some poor invisible animal to shreds. He's kooky. It's why I like him.

I throw my leg over Croc's back and hold on to the golden pole. It's cold and clammy, and it has this metallic smell that reminds me of camping. Which reminds me of my father. But before I can get sad, the ride starts.

As much as I hate roller coasters, I love spinning rides. My parents say I loved to spin myself in circles when I was little, and even though I don't remember doing that, I remember the feeling. I'd turn and turn, and all the hard edges of things would get soft, and the world would become a nice, safe blur. It's the exact same feeling I'm having now as the carousel starts turning.

At first, the music is so slow, I can't recognize the song. In a few seconds, though, Croc is picking up serious speed and the melody starts to sound familiar. The music doesn't have vocals, but I can hear the lyrics in my head:

"Bid your cares goodbye . . .
You can fly! You can fly! You can fly!"

The carousel whips me around, faster and faster until I sort of can't breathe. And just then, I do believe I can fly. I half expect my legs to lift off the stirrups and leave me clutching the pole so I don't float away.

I feel so giddy that I laugh out loud. I throw my head back and laugh and laugh until my cheeks hurt. Then the ride slows down, and I get off.

And then I do it all over again.

★ ★ ★

I ride the carousel eight times in a row, and each time I choose a different animal. For ride number eight, I hop on this weird winged-monkey creature, which reminds me of *The Wizard of Oz*, one of my all-time favorite movies.

As usual, it's all little kids and their parents riding on the carousel, except for this bunch of high schoolers that crowd into the chariot in front of me. They're being really loud, and as I watch, one of them pulls a Sharpie out of his pocket and starts writing on the dashboard of the chariot. I can't see what he's writing, but it's got to be something pretty gross, because his friends are whooping and laughing and shoving him. I look over to the redheaded ride operator, but he's clueless, making sure little kids are strapped in.

"Somethin' funny?" booms a voice.

It's a security guard, a massive security guard. He's standing directly in front of the chariot, wearing a pair of sunglasses with mirrored lenses. He's so tall and thick that his body blots out the sun. He reminds me of a human wall.

Sharpie Boy slips the marker into his pocket and mumbles, "Huh?"

"Sounds like y'all are havin' a grand ol' time over here," the security guard drawls. He has a really gravelly voice. "So I came to see what's so funny. If I was a bettin' man, I'd say it has somethin' to do with that Sharpie in your pocket."

All the kids start talking at once, offering up their own versions of "Sharpie? What Sharpie? I don't know anything about a Sharpie."

The security guard just stands there, his huge arms crossed over his chest. He's wearing a Foreverland Security T-shirt that looks about two sizes too small. I can tell it's on purpose, to show off his huge muscles.

The high schoolers are playing dumb, and it's impossible to tell what the guard's reaction is because his eyes are hidden behind the sunglasses and he's standing there completely still. The only part of him that moves is this vein in the side of his neck, which is throbbing like there's an alien in there trying to escape. That pulsing vein really freaks me out.

He walks around to the side of the chariot, takes off his sunglasses, and leans over so he can read what the kid wrote on the dash. They're all watching him, and they must be getting worried, because they're totally quiet now.

"See now, to me, that don't seem funny," he says,

shaking his head. "Then again, everyone's different. I wonder what the police'll think."

"But we were just playing around," says Sharpie Boy.

"Vandalism," the security guard growls, "is a crime. And crimes get punished."

Everybody on the carousel is watching the scene. Sharpie Boy starts talking fast now, saying he's really sorry and begging the security guy not to call the cops. His voice gets all thin and high, like he's going to start crying. Sharpie Boy is obviously a jerk, but I feel sorry for him. He looks humiliated.

The security guard speaks then, jabbing his finger at each one of them as he spits his words out: "Get. Outta. My. Park."

The kids are on their feet and leaping off the carousel faster than seems humanly possible. The security guard slides his sunglasses over his eyes again and flashes a big smile to the rest of us on the ride. Wow, are his teeth white. They don't even look real, they're so white.

"Sorry 'bout that, folks!"

His voice is friendly now, and relaxed, like an airplane pilot's. He gives us a little wave. "Y'all have a magical day."

I watch as he walks over to Clueless Redhead, who's standing next to the ride's gate. "Cover that with a sticker for now," he says. "We'll get maintenance to repaint tonight."

"Okay, Captain," Clueless Redhead says, but almost sarcastically, like it's not okay at all.

The Captain seems to notice his tone, because he says, "Lemme ask you a question, Jed. You got a problem with your vision? You need glasses?"

"Uhhhh, no."

"No what?"

Jed makes a pained face. "No, *sir*."

"That's what I thought," the Captain says, nodding. "Keep your eyes open, Jed. Eyes. Open. You read me?"

"Yeah, okay," Jed says.

As the Captain walks away, Jed lets loose with a mega eye roll, so big I think he could injure something. He marches over to the chariot and slaps a Foreverland sticker over the graffiti, the whole time muttering under his breath. The only bit I catch is: "fascist Sasquatch."

It doesn't seem like an affectionate nickname.

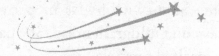

CHAPTER 5

By the time my winged monkey comes to a stop, ending the carousel ride, my stomach is growling wildly. I haven't really had anything to eat today and it's already 3:34, according to my watch. I am starving. And that can only mean one thing: food court.

I am unbelievably excited about hitting the food court. I have waited twelve years for this moment. I've waited twelve years for junk food overload.

There are smaller food courts sprinkled around Foreverland, but toward the middle of the park is a supersized dining area called Magical Morsels. That's where I'm headed.

I zip on over there and am nearly drooling as I read the different menus—cotton candy, slushies, nachos with neon-orange dipping sauce so fake that they have to put the word *cheese* in quotation marks.

Jackpot, I am thinking.

My mother never lets Gwen or me eat this stuff. When we come to the park, she always packs us sandwiches. No frills, either: just turkey breast,

27

maybe some ham, with Swiss or provolone, no mayo, always on multigrain bread. She packs veggie sticks and unsalted pretzels.

Fun fact: Unsalted pretzels are an oxymoron. Like happy dodgeball.

The salt is precisely what makes a pretzel a pretzel. Take it away, and it's just really stale bread.

I am thinking of all the unsalted pretzels I've had to choke down over the years, and this makes me think of Hugh. Or:

Human

Unsalted pretzel, also known as

Gwen's

Honey-pie.

Hugh is the reason my sister stopped hanging out with me. I have no proof of this, but it's the only logical conclusion. It went like this:

Before Hugh: Gwen and Margaret are the best of friends! They fill notebooks with collaborative acrostics. Their life together is like one big shampoo commercial—all slow-motion laughing.

After Hugh: Margaret becomes invisible to Gwen, and all the joy is sucked out of the world.

Thanks, Hugh!

Thinking about Hugh almost ruins my appetite. Almost, but not quite.

I decide to order from Cloud Café because it has a nice ring to it. I'm going to get a Magic Special, which includes a:

1. Magic Dog, aka a foot-long hot dog with "magic" sauce, that looks a lot like cheese. Or, I should say, "cheese."
2. Magic Shake, aka a vanilla milkshake colored blue.
3. Magic Fries, aka regular french fries with the word *magic* printed on the carton.

I'm standing at the back of the line, debating whether I should get nachos, too, when I hear yelling. The cashier, a really short girl who looks about Gwen's age, is shouting at the guy manning the slushie machine. It's kind of funny because she's about a foot smaller than him, but he looks totally terrified of her. To be honest, she *is* pretty terrifying-looking.

Her hair is in a pixie cut that's dyed platinum blonde, but there are long black roots growing in, which make her look tough instead of sweet. She has a lip ring in her bottom lip, which is covered in purple lipstick, and her Foreverland staff T-shirt has been sliced open and put back together in a complicated way that involves a lot of safety pins.

Slushie Guy puts his hands up in an "I surrender" gesture, but this only makes her angrier. The fight looks like it's going to take a while, and by now I'm too hungry to wait, so I head to the next counter, which serves up the same scrumptious delicacies.

I order the Magic Special and then—why not?—Magic Nachos, too, and also—YOLO!—a blue cotton candy. I carry the overloaded tray to the nearest empty seat. Then, I feast.

Sometimes, when you finally get what you've always wanted, it's a letdown.

This was not one of those times.

I polish off the cotton candy, nachos, and fries in about two minutes, and each bite is a revelation. I save the hot dog for last.

Fun fact: I've never eaten a hot dog. Unless you count tofu dogs. Which you really should not.

Hot dogs are one of those things my mom goes nuts about.

"I don't want to rain on your parade," she says.

Umm, really? I think but do not say. *Because that's kind of your specialty.*

"But a person has to draw the line somewhere," she goes on. "And I draw the line at hot dogs. They're not even meat."

Meat or no meat, this hot dog is freakishly delicious. It's salty and oily, and my teeth make the hot-dog skin *snap*! It is so tasty that I don't eat it so much as inhale it.

While I am devouring it like a ravenous wolf, I

think of what my mother's face would look like if she could see me. The expression I imagine—shock! horror! betrayal!—is so hilarious that I laugh out loud. Which is unfortunate.

Laughing = Fun

Eating = Fun

Laughing + Eating = Not Fun

Laughing + Eating = Choking

CHAPTER 6

Choking on the hot dog is a lot less enjoyable than devouring it.

For a second, I think that it's going to be fine, that the enormous hunk of not-even-meat lodged in my throat is going to slip the rest of the way down. But then it doesn't go down, and I realize that I'm actually choking on my first real hot dog.

And I know that it's not the most tragic thing to ever happen in the history of the world—I'm aware there have been catastrophes that are probably a smidge worse, like, say, the atomic bomb going off, but at this moment, I truly feel like this is a tragedy beyond compare.

And I'm also thinking, besides being the most tragic thing, it's probably the most embarrassing. I mean, what am I, three years old?

As the milliseconds tick by, I am way too mortified to get help. But then I try to take a breath, and I don't get any air, and it feels sort of like when I've stayed too long underwater except, oh, a billion times more scary. Suddenly, I'm more scared than I am mortified.

So I start waving my hands around, and right away, I feel something whack me in the back. Hard. So hard that my chest crashes against the table and my milkshake gets knocked over and my tray flies onto the floor. The other thing that flies onto the floor is the gross hunk of hot dog that very nearly killed me.

I gasp for breath, and now, the breath comes. My throat's killing me, there are tears streaming down my face, and I'm really queasy, but I am definitely not choking to death anymore. Which is awesome.

A little crowd has gathered around me. Someone's handing me a cup of water, and somebody else is offering to take me to the first aid station. I didn't even know the park had a first aid station.

There's a curly-haired mom-type lady with a fanny pack standing close to me, and she looks really concerned, so I guess that she is the one who whacked my back.

"Thank you," I say to her. My voice is so hoarse, it surprises me.

"Oh, hon, it wasn't me," she says. She looks around for a second and then says, "Where'd that boy get to? . . . He was just—oh, there he is."

I follow her finger and see a figure standing at the entrance to the Games area. I think I'm having a hallucination brought on by my near-death experience.

It's the waving boy from Pirate's Cove.

I jump to my feet to run over to him, but a

really tall, really skinny man who looks a lot like a scarecrow wearing a Foreverland Security T-shirt steps in front of me. He's saying something into a walkie-talkie about a medical call, requesting assistance.

I'm saying, "No, no, it's okay," but he's not listening to me. He's listening to the walkie-talkie, to a gravelly voice coming out of it that is saying, "Copy that. On my way."

"Have a seat," Scarecrow Guy tells me, not in a mean way, just concerned. "The Captain's coming over to make sure you're okay."

I'm new to the whole runaway thing, so I don't really know how it all works. Still, I'm pretty sure that Rule Number One of Runaways is: Steer clear of the security captain. Especially when he has the muscles and temper of the Incredible Hulk.

Scarecrow Guy must see that my body has launched into panic mode, because he smiles in this reassuring way. "Don't worry, you're not in trouble. In fact, the Captain will probably give you a free meal voucher. It's worth ten dollars."

I shake my head.

"No thanks," I say. It comes out in a whisper, and it hurts my throat so much. But I want this guy to think I'm A-OK, so I clear my throat, trying not to wince, and I say, "I'm totally fine. Honestly. And I'm late? To meet my parents? They, uh, they worry a lot. So I'd better . . . uhhh, skedaddle."

I sling my backpack over my shoulder, making a mental note to never, *ever* use the word *skedaddle* again. Then I quickly weave through the little crowd, toward Games.

As I walk away, I hear the crackle of a walkie-talkie behind me and Scarecrow Guy's voice canceling the request for assistance.

So that's one crisis avoided. Two, if you count almost dying from the hot dog.

By the time I get to the spot where the waving boy was standing, he's gone. But on the floor is something that catches my attention. At first it just looks like garbage, but when I crouch, I see it's not. It's some kind of origami—a crane or a frog, I can't really tell, but I can tell it's supposed to be something. I pick it up and then walk into the Games area to see if I can find Mystery Boy aka Waving Boy aka Back Whacker. I wander around for a while, but I don't see him anywhere.

So I sit down on a bench across from a Skee-Ball game. I sit there for a long time, or what feels like a long time, anyway. I just sit and watch people try to toss loud, heavy balls into the holes. Mostly, they miss.

I take out my notebook and write:

Hazardous

Object

That is

Deadly, if
Only to this
Girl.

Then I look at the origami creation I found. I examine it for long enough that I finally figure out what it's supposed to be. Not a crane or a frog. It's a flying saucer.

I look at it closely and see that it's not made from regular paper but from a folded Foreverland map. As I'm turning the UFO over, one of the feet comes loose, and when I try to fold it back up, another foot gets unfolded. The more I fiddle with it, the more it comes apart.

I am thinking that I ruined it when my eye catches sight of a bright red mark on the map. I unfold the paper all the way, and there, in the middle, is a big red *X*.

X marks the spot.

CHAPTER 7

The *X* marking the spot is in Sky City—on a ride called the Starship.

I love the Starship.

When I see that the *X* marks the Starship, I get really excited. I should be freaked out by the whole thing, but I am not. Before I've even thought it over, I'm at the entrance to the ride, shoving my backpack in one of the cubbies where you can stash your belongings. I look around for Mystery Boy, but I don't see him anywhere. So I walk up the steps into the Starship.

There are still a bunch of empty seats left. I mean, they're not seats really, because you don't sit down. One of the cool things about the Starship is you ride it standing up. There are no straps or belts or anything, which seems like it'd be really dangerous. But you don't need them. Centrifugal force is your seat belt. I learned about it in science last year.

I head to an open spot on the wall and lean back to wait. For what, I'm not sure.

I check my watch, like Mystery Boy and I have

an actual meeting time, which of course we do not. It's 5:21.

I watch the second hand *tick tick tick*, which is something I find very relaxing. This is part of why I wear a watch, even though I don't really need one since the time's always on my phone. I just like checking the time on a watch. I also like playing music on a record player and reading books made of paper. I like old stuff better.

And now my watch comes in handy because when I left home, I also left my phone. If I hadn't, my parents would've tracked me down in five minutes.

I watch the second hand of my watch until it reaches the twelve, then I look up and, like magic, Mystery Boy is there, in the spot next to me.

The first thing I notice is his hair. It's pretty hard to ignore. It is thick and really dark and wavy and it falls over one eye, which makes Mystery Boy look even more mysterious.

The eye I can see is as dark as his hair, the kind of eye you can see your own reflection in.

"Hey," he says to me, smiling. He has the widest grin I've ever seen. It makes his whole face seem like it's smiling.

"Hi," I croak.

"What's up?"

He says it like we're old friends, like we were just chatting a few minutes ago.

The correct answer to this question is: "You tell me. You're the one who invited me here."

But instead of saying this, I am acting like nothing's weird and saying, "Um, not much?"

"Does your throat hurt? Man, that was wild, how fast you ate that hot dog. You training for a hot-dog-eating contest or something?"

The correct answer to this is: "Thank you for saving my life. Also, who are you?"

But all I'm saying is "Uh."

He smiles his whole-face grin again. "Do you ever use words with more than one syllable?"

"Frequently."

"*Aha!* Nice. Good. Because I am so bored. Are you bored out of your mind? Or is it me? I can't even tell anymore."

I have no idea how to respond to this, because no, I'm not bored, and seriously, how could anyone be bored here? It's an *amusement* park. It is basically the cure for boredom. That could be Foreverland's slogan. So I don't know how to reply to Mystery Boy. But it turns out I don't have to, because at that moment the Starship starts moving.

It starts slow but picks up speed really fast. My instinct is to grab ahold of something, but there's nothing to hold on to, and anyway, I can't move a muscle. The speed of the ride is pressing my body against the cushioned panel, lifting my feet off the ground a little. I feel like I'm glued in place.

I lie totally still—well, still while spinning around at super-speed—and I stare straight ahead, until I see some flicker out of the corner of my eye that makes me turn my head.

Mystery Boy is not lying still. He's sucked flat against the wall, like me, but he's shimmying sideways, so that his body is perpendicular to mine. He looks like a minus sign. Mystery Boy crosses one ankle in front of the other, then bends his arms and puts his hands behind his head, so he looks like he's sunbathing by the pool. Then he shimmies back to his starting position, and I think he's done.

He's not done. He's just getting warmed up.

He bends his knees so that the soles of his feet are pressed flat against the wall, and then he lunges forward and grabs the big steering wheel thing that's in the middle of the Starship.

This makes me really nervous. For all I know, he can get sucked into some kind of black hole that might pull him into its vortex and spit him out who knows where.

And I didn't run away to live in an amusement park to witness the tragic death of a mysterious boy.

But there's nothing I can do to stop him, since I feel like I'm suctioned to the wall, totally frozen. So I watch as he rides like this, his feet pressed against the wall, his hands on the steering wheel, looking down toward the floor of the ride. And then he lets go of the wheel.

The wind is making his T-shirt ripple wildly like a skydiver's, but he's not falling. His arms are stretched out at his sides, and just like a tightrope walker, he's perfectly balanced.

I don't know how he's doing this. I mean, I know it must be physics. But it doesn't feel like physics. It feels like magic.

I'm waiting for someone to stop him because he is definitely breaking a dozen rules, but the whole trick only lasts a few seconds. Then he leans back and lets himself be suctioned to the wall again, in one swift motion. Seconds after that, the ride starts to slow.

I can't even really tell when the ride has stopped, because my head is still spinning. I shut my eyes and let the dizziness pass. When I open them, the boy is gone.

CHAPTER 8

I manage to pry myself from the wall and stumble out of the ride, still a little off-balance. I have a lot of questions. Why'd Mystery Boy invite me here just to suddenly vanish into thin air? Why's he following me around? How did he do that freaky trick on the Starship?

But the only person who can answer these questions is Mystery Boy himself, who's gone. So I go back to the spot in Games where I found the UFO, hoping he might have left something else there—another message maybe. I look all over the floor and even behind the coin machine. Nothing.

I stand there, trying to figure out my next move. The coin machine has a big digital sign—one word in red letters that blinks on and off.

CHANGE
CHANGE
CHANGE

I know this is meant as a noun, like *coins*, but it

feels like a verb. It's like this machine is screaming at me, *"Change! Right now! Be different!"*

And sure, why not? Everybody around me is changing. Gwen's miles away even when we're in the same room. Priya, formerly known as Best Friend Forever, stopped responding to my messages for no apparent reason. And Dad . . . Dad's a totally different person. So either he changed, like, *completely*, or I never really knew him, which is even scarier.

Yep, everyone around me is unrecognizable. So why not me, too?

CHANGE
CHANGE
CHANGE

My hypnotic state is interrupted by a little kid behind me who taps my arm and asks, "Are you using the machine?"

"Yes," I say, surprising myself.

I do use it. I insert a ten-dollar bill and get a huge pile of quarters to use at the arcade.

Fun fact: This is my first time playing video games.

Related fact: I love video games.

I love *Super Mario*. I love *Galaga*. And I totally love *Pac-Man*.

I can see why people get hooked on video games. It's like hitting pause on your life. You can't think of anything while you're playing, because if you want to zap those ghosts or win the grand prix, your brain needs to focus all its attention on doing that and only that.

I use all my quarters, then go back, put in another ten dollars and use all *those* quarters, too. I know I'm burning through my money and I should slow down before it's all gone. I felt rich this morning when I counted out the $182 I've stockpiled after a year of tutoring the little girl that lives next door. But after a round-trip Metro-North train ticket and admission to Foreverland, I had enough left to buy food for a while—a week, maybe, if I'm careful with my spending. I definitely don't have video game money. I know this. But I also know that right now, more than anything in the world, I really, really, really want to win the big Saint Bernard stuffed animal that is calling out to me from inside the claw-grabber machine.

"*Graaaaaab meeeeee!*" it calls. "*I'm riiiiiiight here on top of the piiiiiiiile!*"

I insert another five dollars bill into the *CHANGE* machine and promptly lose all of it in the claw machine. The Saint Bernard is so big, and it's right in the middle, so it seems like there is no way to miss it. And yet I do, every time. So I march over to a bench and write an angry acrostic.

Got to be a

Racket, this

Asinine machine, guzzling

Buckets and

Buckets of quarters, and

Every time, you end up a lose-

R.

If Gwen were here, she'd disqualify the acrostic because of the ending. She's a stickler. She's also the one who taught me to write acrostics in the first place. It was our thing for a long time—until she got a whole bunch of other things, like a boyfriend and a swim team to captain.

I scribble another angry acrostic:

Girl

Wonder

Effortlessly

Nailing it.

My pen suddenly gets knocked out of my hand, thanks to a plush projectile that has landed on my lap. It's the Saint Bernard from the claw grabber.

I look up. Standing in front of me is Mystery Boy.

"What are you writing?" he asks. He tilts his head sideways to try to make out the words in my notebook. I feel totally exposed and slam the notebook shut.

"Is it for school? Like, summer homework?"

"No," I reply, offended that he thinks I'm the kind of person who'd be doing homework at an amusement park. "It's an acrostic."

"Sounds like a medical condition." His mouth erupts into that enormous smile. "Do you see a doctor for that?"

"No," I answer. "I don't see a doctor. I mean, I *do* see a doctor, you know, for annual checkups or whatever, but not for that. I mean, it's not a medical condition. It's a, umm, a poem? But the first letter of every line spells a word? Vertically?"

He doesn't say anything, which is unfortunate because it gives me time to think about the mess of words that just poured out of my mouth. I wonder, for the millionth time, why my particular style of nervous has to be the Talk-Too-Much kind. I consider taking a vow of silence. Hey, it works for the monks.

Mystery Boy jams a hand inside the pocket of his cargo shorts and pulls out a yo-yo. It's a blue yo-yo with the words *Where magic never ends!* written on one side and a big golden star on the other.

"So there's a word hidden in the poem?" he asks. "Like a code."

He winds the yo-yo up, fast and sure, without even looking at it.

"Sort of, I mean, I guess? I, uhh, never thought of it that way." I pick up the Saint Bernard so it's sitting on my lap. "Hey, how did you—I mean, thanks for the dog."

He doesn't reply. Instead, he flicks his wrist and the yo-yo shoots out. It shoots straight down and zips back up. It looks like the blue tongue of a lizard darting out to grab an insect. It's so fast, if you blinked you'd miss it. He does it again, and another time.

"Read me one," he says.

"One what?"

He flicks his wrist again, and now the yo-yo is making a loop, then another loop, and the golden star on the side is spinning so fast, it looks like it's twinkling. It is totally mesmerizing.

Then suddenly, the yo-yo snaps back into his palm and he shoves it into his pocket.

"Read me one of your poems. Your favorite."

He plops down next to me on the bench.

I scooch away instinctively.

"No."

"Why not? I mean, it's not classified information, right?"

"Forget it. No way."

"It's just a poem. What's the big deal?"

"There's no big deal. I just don't want to."

He shrugs like he's dropping the subject, but then his hand darts out and grabs the notebook right out of my lap.

"Thanks . . ." he says, and then, reading the cover where my name is written, he adds, "Margaret. Thanks, Margaret."

"Give. It. Back," I growl. I can tell by the look on his face that he's surprised by how ferocious I sound. He's not the only one.

He stops smiling and hands it back to me.

"I was just playing."

I unzip my backpack and shove the notebook in there.

"I'm sorry," he says. "For real."

"Congratulations," I shoot back, standing up.

"Hey, wait up," he says, walking after me as I make my way out of Games. "Hey, I didn't get to introduce myself."

"Too bad," I say, without looking at him.

"Jaime," he says. "I'm Jaime."

I turn around to face him.

"You mean your name isn't Weird Stalker Dude?"

"Well, that's my *last* name," he says. "My first name's Jaime."

I tilt my head to the side and stare at him, speechless. I'm furious because grabbing my notebook was seriously a jerk move. But also, I'm curious. I have a lot of questions, more every minute I spend with him. So I can't figure out if I should tell him to leave me alone—I mean it—or ask him to teach me the claw-grabber trick, please.

But it turns out I don't have to decide, because while I am standing there, staring at him, he says, "Later," spins on his heel, and jogs away.

I look down at the Saint Bernard, which is still in my hands.

"Toto," I say, "I've a feeling we're not in Kansas anymore."

CHAPTER 9

My throat still kind of hurts from the Hot Dog of Doom incident, so I decide to get an ice cream. I don't feel like showing my face back at Magical Morsels, but the wonderful thing about amusement parks is that they are chock-full of ice cream stands. I only have to wander around Waterworld for a minute or two before I find one.

I order a cone of vanilla-chocolate swirl.

"Chocnilla," Gwen and I used to call it. "For the girl who wants it all!"

Gwen doesn't eat ice cream anymore. She eats Greek yogurt. Apparently, it's *just* as tasty and *so* much better for you. Hugh agrees. Which is not really saying much, because I've never heard Hugh disagree with anything.

I plop down on a bench and let the creamy, sugary, non-Greek-yogurt-y goodness slide down my raw throat. A little girl in long pigtails walks by, holding a gigantic ice cream cone that looks as big as her head. She has just gotten her hands on this ice cream, hasn't even taken her first lick, and the look of anticipation on her face is hilarious. Take the joy of a snow day, add in the excitement of Christmas morning, and top it off with the thrill of getting a puppy for your birthday, and you get the look on this girl's face. She sticks out her tiny tongue to take the first lick, but she licks too hard, and the entire pile of ice cream falls off the cone and starts to melt on the hot pavement.

Horror! Rage! Despair! And then tears, so many tears. It looks like she will never be happy again. Then her mom says, "We'll get you a new one," and just like that, presto! Everything is all better.

I think about how things would be so much easier if I could be five again, or ten, or even eleven. Sometimes I wish I didn't have to grow up, because the older I get, the more complicated and screwed up everything seems to get. I don't understand why everyone around me is in such a big rush to get older. It's like they just want to fast-forward through the last bit of being a kid to get to the good stuff. Or the stuff they *think* is going to be good, anyway. And if they can't make themselves get older faster, then they'll just act older, by cursing and drinking coffee and wearing tons of eyeliner. I blame puberty.

Fun fact: I am not a fan of puberty.

First of all, we need a better word for it. Priya and I used to joke that *puuuuuberty* sounds gross. It's right up there with *pustule*. The way it's described in books and health class makes me feel like it's an alien invasion.

I finish off my chocnilla cone and scribble an acrostic in my notebook.

Pimples,

Underarm hair, and

Boobs, oh my!

Even the word is

Really gross. I'll

Take a rain check, thank

You.

I like this acrostic. I think Gwen would like it, too.

I slide my notebook into my backpack and take stock of the things I packed this morning, stuff I thought would come in handy. I've got:

1. Three mini hand sanitizer bottles—green apple, orange Creamsicle, and lavender.
2. Change of clothes.
3. Sunscreen, SPF 50.
4. Flashlight with extra set of AA batteries.
5. Ziploc bag containing toothbrush, toothpaste, and hairbrush.
6. Paperback copies of *The Wonderful Wizard of Oz*, *Alice's Adventures in Wonderland*, and *Peter Pan*.
7. Wallet containing fifty-two dollars in

bills, some change, and a Metro-North ticket back to Grand Central.

8. Rabbit foot charm hanging off the zipper, for good luck.
9. A plush pink bunny, aka Darling.

I'll admit, Darling's not practical. I almost didn't bring her. I figured that if I'm old enough to run away, I probably should be old enough to leave my lovey at home. So I left her on my bed, right next to my cell phone.

But as I was walking out the door, past the big red suitcase, I changed my mind. I went back for Darling. I made her into a Runaway Bunny.

When I was a kid, that story seemed nice, but when you stop to think about it, that mom is kind of a stalker. Like, no matter what that bunny does, she can't escape her mom. Honestly, that bunny needs a restraining order.

Suddenly, from some other corner of the park, there's the sound of drums and trumpets and stuff. A marching band. Then the low rumble of a far-off crowd cheering. I check my watch.

8:03.

The Twilight Parade.

CHAPTER 10

Every night in the summer, at eight, Foreverland has a big parade. My family always went, every year. It's cheesy but fun. They don't have floats or anything, but the staff dresses up in costumes—pirates, knights, fairies, mermaids, princesses—and there's a marching band.

The part Gwen and I used to like was how the parade people throw free stuff out at the crowd, Mardi Gras–style—beaded necklaces, cardboard crowns, plastic rings. Once I even caught a magic wand. Then they end the parade with a big finish, which is the band playing "You Can Fly!" And as the grand finale, all the parade people throw huge handfuls of pixie dust at the crowd. It's just blue glitter, but still, I've always loved it.

Tonight, the parade comes at a perfect time. Not because I'm going, but because everyone else is. Which means I can look for a place to hide without too many people around. The park closes at ten, so I have a little bit of time, but not much.

On the train this morning, I brainstormed a few ideas for hideouts, but the best one I could think of was hiding in a stall in the women's restroom.

On the one hand, there are plenty of restrooms to choose from. But I worry that a bathroom is the kind of place that security always checks, as part of their nightly routine. Also, what if I get locked in the bathroom for the night? I definitely don't want to be at home right now, but sleeping on a toilet sounds worse, if that's possible.

So I need a better option. I start walking around the park, on the lookout for the perfect hiding spot. I'm not worried. I know I'll find one.

Fun fact: I am an expert hider.

When I was younger, I loved to hide. I'd stay hidden for a really, really long time. Like, too long.

My favorite place to hide was the hall closet. It was narrow, like all our closets, but weirdly deep, with two rods for coats—one rod in front of the other. When I read about the wardrobe that's a gateway to another world in *The Lion, the Witch and the Wardrobe*, I thought of that hall closet. I always had to push really hard against the weight of all the furry, feathery, leathery coat bottoms to get in. Then I'd creep over the sneakers and rain boots and umbrellas until I got to the very back. There was an old can of paint back there, and it made a good seat.

I'd sit on the paint can, in the pitch black, and wait for someone to notice I was gone. I loved the way it smelled in there—woodsy, from the cedar mothballs. I always hated the real woods, which are full of bears and disease-carrying ticks, but I liked the woods smell. What I really liked, though, was hearing my mom's voice get louder and more panicked.

"Margaret? . . . Margaret! . . . MARgaret!!! Are you in here? You'd better get your butt out of wherever you're hiding, or you are going to be in big trouble. MARGARET!"

I never got in real trouble for hiding, though. My mom was always so relieved when I appeared that her anger melted away.

As I look for a hiding place in Foreverland, I think about this and I can't help wondering what my parents are doing at home. It's after eight, so they've probably all been home for a while, and by now they must've found my note. I left it on the kitchen counter, where they'd be sure to find it. It was in the form of an acrostic.

Getting

Out

Of here.

Don't worry, I'll

Be back someday.

You all

Enjoy your Last Supper.

The Last Supper part was a tad dramatic, I'll admit. But, seriously, that's exactly what it was—our last supper together. And even though I know that running away to live in an amusement park wasn't the best response to this, I still think that forcing us to sit at the table and make small talk, the whole time knowing it's the last time—I don't know, that seems either really dumb or really cruel, and either way, I'm not up for it.

I don't find a hiding place in Waterworld or Sky City, either. I head toward Magic Mile and pass the parade, which is in full swing. I stand at the back of the crowd and watch a very bored-looking king throw necklaces into the crowd. I'm pretty sure he's the kid who was working the turnstiles this morning. His long hair is pulled back into a ponytail, and his shoulders are slumped way over as he shuffles along. He could not look more uninterested. He's not even looking at the crowd as he tosses the plastic jewels at us. It's hilarious and, actually, the only part of this getup that makes him look actually royal. In real life, royal people must be bored all the time.

His Royal Highness tosses a foam sword at the crowd on the side of the parade opposite me. It's a big-ticket item—all the kids are lunging for it. And there, in the middle of the action, is Jaime. He raises his arm straight up, opens his hand, and the sword lands right in his palm, like the king threw it directly at him. His mouth breaks into his massive smile, and he looks across the parade, through the crowd, directly at me. He bows his head, like he's saying "m'lady." I hold my hands up high and clap for him, playing the part of the princess for a minute. I don't know how I keep running into him like this, but by now, I'm not surprised.

There are a bunch of little kids standing around Jaime who look really disappointed that they didn't catch the sword, and he must notice, because he turns to one of them—a tiny boy with a big head of curly hair—and says something to him. Then he lowers the foam sword down onto each of the boy's shoulders, like he's knighting him. When he's done, he hands the boy the sword. As the boy shouts with glee, Jaime shrinks back and vanishes into the crowd.

I take off, too, farther into Magic Mile, because I still have nowhere to hide when the park closes. I walk past the Majestic Theater, where they do magic shows during the day, and then I walk by the Haunted House.

I've gone to the Haunted House every year since the very first time we came to Foreverland. Even though I'm terrified of my own shadow half the time, I have never been scared of monsters. This never made any sense to my mom, but it's simple. I'm only scared of stuff that's real, like tornadoes, defective roller coasters, divorce.

So I'm not scared of haunted houses. In fact, I

love them. I decide to forget my search for a minute and go inside.

The Haunted House is nothing fancy, just a square brown house with a red triangle roof. The whole thing is pretty cheesy. It doesn't even have real people in it, just animatronic figures.

I walk under the big sign that says HAUNTED HOUSE in orange letters that look like they're melting. A teenager in a park T-shirt is standing by the entrance, counting the number of people that go in. She has black hair with big blue streaks in the front, and she's put her hair into two braids, except her hair's really short, so they are the shortest braids I've ever seen.

I step into a dark room that I remember from all the times I've come. The air-conditioning is on full blast, and it is nice and cool. The room is really dark—the only light is pointed down on an old-fashioned painting of a Victorian lady in a blue dress.

The teenager says "Good to go" into a walkie-talkie and then closes the door to the entrance. Within a minute, creepy piano music starts playing from a speaker over my head. Then comes a man's deep voice. With a British accent, of course.

Fun fact: Fictional villains always talk in British accents.

If I were British, I might be offended.

"Welcome, guests, to my humble abode. I do

hope you don't startle easily. There are some—
ahem—unusual creatures in residence here."

Then the creepy piano music comes back, all
minor chords, like in a horror movie. The light
above the old-fashioned painting flickers to get our
attention, and then the eyes in the painting move
from side to side. It's dumb and predictable, but I
love it anyway.

The British villain voice goes on. "No flash
photography, please. It disturbs the creatures, and
when they're disturbed, well, there's no telling what
they'll do."

Then all the lights go off, and the voice breaks
through the darkness saying, "Are you quite
ready?" Cue the creepy chuckle. "Well then, come
on in, won't you? We won't bite. Except, maybe,
Florinda."

The chuckle gets louder and louder and louder,
and then there's a huge explosion of sound, like all
the piano keys are getting hit at the same time. Then
bam! The light above the painting turns back on
suddenly, only the painting is gone and in its place
is a skeleton wearing the lady's blue dress. Her jaws
clamp together and move apart, and all the while the
piano keys clang. A little kid in front of me screams
his head off.

And I don't know why, but I feel more relaxed
than I have in a long time.

CHAPTER 11

The Haunted House has not changed one bit since the last time I came. The British villain narrates, and there's a little animatronic act in each room. In the living room, a skeleton bride and groom waltz; in the kitchen, a mad scientist brings Frankenstein to life; in the bedroom, Dracula jumps out from under the covers; and in the dining room, zombies feast on a bowl of human brains.

I like the tour so much I do it again, and then a third time. As I walk in for my third tour, I hear Tiny Braid Girl say into her walkie-talkie: "Uuuugh. How can there still be a half hour until closing? I'm so sick of this crap."

Which is when I realize the park is closing soon and I still don't have a hiding spot.

The tour's already started, so I walk through, trying to drum up more ideas for places to hide. I come back to the women's bathroom and decide it's not so bad. I remind myself there are worse things than sleeping upright on a public toilet. Even if I can't think of any.

Since it's my third time walking through the

Haunted House, this time I don't look at the animatronic monsters that you're supposed to watch. I look at the little details in each room—the stuff you usually don't notice. Each room has real furniture and accessories, like real curtains on the windows, real pots on the stove, real pillows on the bed.

I'm standing next to the bed where Dracula is about to pop up any minute, and all I can think about are those soft, fluffy pillows. I'm suddenly so tired. Exhausted. All I want to do is crawl into that bed.

That's when I have a brain wave.

I'm going to sleep in the Haunted House.

At just that moment, the music explodes out of the speakers and animatronic Dracula pops up, making a grown woman next to me yelp in surprise. They're all staring at Dracula, but I'm checking out the bottom of the bed. There's a long bed skirt that hangs down to the floor, which covers whatever is— or is not—under the bed.

Then, like always, the room goes totally dark, which is our cue to move on to the next room.

My heart is racing, and my mind is racing, too. This is perfect. This could not be more perfect.

I'll take the last tour of the night through the Haunted House, and when we get to the bedroom, as soon as the room goes dark, I'll drop down and slide under the bed skirt. It'll be pitch-dark, and everyone will be looking forward into the dining room, so no one will notice. If someone does spot me, I'll pretend I tripped or dropped something or whatever.

The only problem is that I have no idea what's under the bed. Could be chain saws under there. Rats. Brown recluse spiders. Dysentery germs. Worries pop up in my brain like moles in a Whac-A-Mole game. I try to knock them down, but they're coming too quick.

I'll get cut. I'll get bit. I'll get dysentery. What do they do when they catch runaways?

Fun fact: There's no way I can do this.

Related fact: There's nothing else I can do.

When the tour's over, I walk quickly to the nearest ladies' room to use the bathroom, and then I'm back at the Haunted House, lining up for the last tour.

CHAPTER 12

I make sure I'm in the back of the tour group. My heart is pounding wildly as we watch the skeletons waltz. By the time Frankenstein comes to life on the kitchen table, the blood is thundering in my ears. Then we get to the bedroom, and the British villain is saying, "How rude of me. You must be terribly fatigued after the long day you've had."

It's weird, but I feel like he's talking directly to me. I *am* terribly fatigued.

"Why not retire for the evening?" he purrs.

I know that in about ten seconds, Dracula's going to pop up, and then it's go time. My heart is slamming against my chest like it wants to bust through.

Music blares.

Dracula appears.

Gasps.

Laughing.

Every muscle in my body is ready, tense. Then it's suddenly dark, and without even thinking, I'm crouching, and then I'm crawling like a soldier, on my belly. I slide my backpack off my shoulders, shoving it through the bed skirt, and then I'm under, too.

I'm holding my breath, waiting for someone to yell "Hey!" or "Excuse me!" or something a lot less polite. But no one yells anything. All the sounds I can hear are coming from the next room, where the zombies are being introduced to the crowd.

I reach for my backpack to make sure it's pulled all the way under the bed. As I'm groping in the dark, my hand brushes against something long and ropy.

An anaconda. A python. A boa constrictor.

I brace myself for fangs and venom and sudden death. Or maybe not so sudden. I don't know that much about snakes, and I really have no idea whether you die instantly or slowly, which, obviously, is way, way worse.

I'm starting to pray for swift death when I realize in all the seconds I've been freaking out, the supposed python hasn't moved at all. So I screw up the courage to touch it and, of course, it's just a tangle of electrical cords. I push them over to make more space for myself, and then I settle in, lying on my stomach, resting my cheek on the back of my hand so my face doesn't touch the dysentery-covered floor.

I listen to the sounds of the tour's big finish in the dining room. I hear everyone walk out, laughing and chatting. It's quiet for a few seconds, and then bright overhead light floods into the room.

There is a little gap in between the floor and the bottom of the bed skirt, and if I squint, I can see a sliver of someone's feet walking around. The feet are wearing lime-green Converse, and the laces of one shoe are untied. That shoelace drives me nuts, like an itch I can't scratch.

The lime-green Converse go in and out of my line of vision, and then another set of footsteps is added into the mix, and a pair of flip-flop-wearing feet enter the room.

I hear thuds that sound like cabinets being banged shut and scraping sounds like chairs being pushed around.

"We need to, like, fast-track this tonight," says the voice attached to the Converse. I recognize the voice. It's Tiny Braid Girl. "Jed's waiting for me."

"When is Jed *not* waiting for you?" says the voice attached to the flip-flops. She has a really nasal tone, like she's got a cold.

"I know," says Tiny Braid Girl, giggling. I hear a swishing sound, which turns out to be a broom brushing across the linoleum floor.

Tiny Braid Girl's voice gets all sweet and sing-songy. "Jed's the best, right? I swear to God, if he wasn't here, I would be out of this dump in a heart-beat. I mean, who needs this crap? Sweeping up Doritos crumbs? Because these spoiled brats can't, like, stop eating Doritos for a second?"

"It's seriously so gross. Last week, I found an enormous cockroach in the kitchen. Like, seriously? As big as my hand."

I squirm around. The cockroach talk makes my whole body tense up. Let's face it, I am in prime cockroach real estate. Anacondas? Unlikely. Cockroaches? Duh.

"People are freaks," Tiny Braid Girl says. She's a fast talker and a fast sweeper, too. She's jabbing the broom ferociously, and when she sticks it under the bed, it goes in far, almost hitting me. "Oh my God, speaking of freaks, did you see that one girl who did the tour, like, eight times?"

"Yeah, I did! She was by herself, too. It was so weird."

That's when I realize they're talking about me.

"It's like, I get riding the Shooting Star seven times in a row because that's awesome or whatever, but this is so cheesy, and if you see it once, it's one time too many."

"People are freaks," Flip-Flop Girl repeats slowly and seriously, like she's some kind of ancient philosopher.

Then they move into the kitchen, where I can't really hear what they are saying.

After what feels like an eternity, I see the flip-flops walking through the room again, a garbage bag dragging behind them.

"Hey, don't forget to kill the lights this time!" she yells to Tiny Braid Girl. "The Captain is gonna fire us if we leave them on again."

"Whatever," snorts Tiny Braid Girl. "He'd be doing us a favor."

Click. The lights going off. All of them.

Slam. The door closing.

Then, quiet.

CHAPTER 13

Fun fact: Places that aren't scary get scary in a hurry when you are alone in the dark.

The cheesy, harmless Haunted House is now giving me goose bumps so intense that I may require medical attention. Here, under the bed in the darkness, I even half believe that zombies and vampires and ghosts are real. The dark does that. It's like a key that unlocks the door to your worst imaginings.

As soon as I hear the door slam, I want to crawl out from under the bed and switch all the lights back on. I don't, of course. That's a rookie move. What if Flip-Flop Girl forgot her phone or keys or wallet, or Tiny Braid Girl left her special comb that she uses to make such tiny braids? You don't have to watch too many scary movies to figure out rule number one of not getting murdered: Never assume the coast is clear.

So I force myself to count to two hundred, and then I inch my way out carefully. My whole body is aching from keeping still for so long, so I toss my backpack on the bed and stretch for a minute.

I walk over to the window of the bedroom. It's

a real window, covered by blackout curtains. Very carefully, I pull the corner of the curtain back just the tiniest bit. My eyes blink back the light.

Outside, there are so many super-bright flood-lights on, it looks like the middle of the day. I get startled by the sound of an engine and then, in the distance, I see a blue pickup truck with MAINTENANCE on the sides. A security golf cart zooms by, headed in the direction of Sky City. Two women roll cleaning carts toward the Majestic entrance. There's all kinds of stuff going on here.

"So I guess I'm in for the night," I say out loud. For some reason, the sound of my own voice makes me feel less scared.

I know I can't turn on the overhead lights, because that'll attract too much attention. But there's a little lamp on the nightstand near the bed that doesn't look like it'll be very bright. I reach under the lampshade and twist the little knob, not really expecting it to work, but it does, and suddenly I can see the outline of things again.

I notice a silky black-and-red men's robe hang-ing on a hook next to the bed. It's old-fashioned, Gothic-style, for Dracula. A smoking jacket, I think, is what you call it. I slip it on over my T-shirt and shorts. Then I knock off my sandals, which slide under the bed, and slip my dirty feet into Drac's leather slippers. They're big but comfortable.

"Hope you don't mind if I make myself at

home," I say to Drac. He is sitting up in the bed, facing me, fangs bared.

"Ahhh, I get it. You're the strong, silent type. That's cool. I am, too. I mean, usually I am. Right now, for some reason, I am really chatty."

I rifle through my backpack for my notebook and pen, and then I walk into the living room, where I turn on a standing lamp in the corner. The armchair right next to the lamp is made of a red velvety material, and I sink right into it.

I find my spot in the notebook easily because I'm using my old family photo as a bookmark. I pull my legs up under me and write:

Devilishly handsome
Rascal, spends lots of time
Alone, which
Causes
Understandable
Loneliness
And that's why he's a little strange.

I write a bunch more acrostics, until my stomach starts rumbling. I realize I haven't eaten anything in hours, since the ice cream cone. Maybe Flip-Flop Girl and Tiny Braid Girl stash some snacks in here somewhere, to nibble on during shifts. And since

I'm already borrowing Drac's clothes, I might as well raid his snack drawer.

I stick the photo back in the notebook and slide the book into the huge silky pocket of the smoking jacket.

If I were Tiny Braid Girl, where would I keep my tiny snacks? I wonder. The kitchen, maybe? I poke around in the cabinets, but no dice.

"You've got a real bachelor pad here," I call to Drac. "Empty cupboards and all that."

I decide to check the closet in the kitchen. I'm just starting to look around in there when I hear the front door of the Haunted House slam.

An electric jolt of shock runs through me. It's so sudden and intense, I feel like I've short-circuited. But then I am moving, stepping all the way into the closet and pulling the door closed behind me, praying it doesn't creak.

I don't hear a creak. I do hear footsteps.

My first thought is: *monsters*.

Like, actual monsters. Real mummies and vampires and zombies. The kind I didn't believe in until, oh, three seconds ago.

The footsteps are heavy and headed right toward the kitchen.

I don't believe in spooks, I tell myself. *I don't believe in spooks.*

I do believe in serial killers, though.

The footsteps get louder, and my legs start to

shake—like actually shake, enough that I worry I'm going to bump into a mop or something and make noise.

Then I hear the beep of a walkie-talkie, and a gruff voice says, "Captain to base. Do you copy?"

At first, I'm flooded with relief. It's just security.

And then, a second later, the relief vanishes: It's *security*. And not just any security guard, either—it's the Captain, with the huge muscles and the mirrored sunglasses. I recognize his drawl. If he was ready to call the cops on that kid for a little graffiti, who knows what he'll do when he finds me here. I'm definitely trespassing, possibly also breaking and entering. I'm wearing Drac's robe and slippers, so maybe that's stealing, too.

A voice comes over the walkie-talkie: "Schmidt to Captain. I copy."

"I'm at Double H," says the Captain. "Those pinheads left the lights on again."

"Yessir. It *is* the second time this summer they did that."

"It's the fourth," says the Captain, his voice dripping with disgust. "I told you to keep a record of the staff's infractions. But maybe you're too busy playin' that video game to follow direct orders."

"No, Captain. Absolutely not, sir. I did that, what you said. A record. I can't find it just at this minute, but—"

Suddenly, the little sliver of light at the bottom

of the closet door turns to black. He must've turned off the living room lamp. Then there's the sound of heavy footsteps moving away, in the direction of the bedroom.

Time slows down as I realize what's about to happen. It hasn't happened yet, but there's nothing I can do to stop it anyway. It's like when you knock a glass off a table and you think, *I need to catch that*, but your body's not as fast as your brain, so you just watch as the thing crashes to the ground and shatters.

My backpack. On the bed.

It takes exactly five seconds for the Captain to find it.

I hear the beep of the walkie-talkie again, then: "Captain to base. I found somethin' here. A backpack."

"Copy that. A guest must've left it."

It's quiet for a few seconds, and I rack my brain to remember if I had ID in the backpack—anything with my name or my picture on it.

Darling. She's in there.

So is my change of clothes and my flashlight.

And my money. All my money. Which may end up being a bit of a problem. I brought the money for food. And I'm already hungry.

Still, there was nothing in my wallet but the money, so I don't think there's anything that links the backpack to me, unless they can do fingerprint analysis on stuffed animals.

Schmidt's voice comes through the walkie-talkie: "I'll tell the girls they need to do a full sweep tomorrow night after guests leave. No shortcuts."

"Unless it wasn't a guest who left the backpack," replies the Captain.

"Whaddya mean? I mean, yessir?"

"I mean, maybe our Boy Wonder's still here."

Right away, I know they are talking about him. Mystery Boy. Back Whacker. Jaime.

"You think so, Captain?" says Schmidt. "I'm pretty sure we ran him out. It's probably just a guest who left it there."

"Sure," says the Captain. "Except . . ."

"Yeah? I mean, except what, sir?"

"Dracula's robe's gone. The slippers, too."

I feel this icy shiver that makes me tremble, like my blood is actually freezing in my veins.

"Uh-huh, gotcha," I hear Schmidt say. "That sounds like him. I'll tell the team to be on the lookout."

I hear the little click of a table lamp turning off. Then the footsteps get louder for a few seconds, and then softer and softer, until finally, the front door slams and it's quiet.

I count to two hundred again, then creep out of the closet. I can't see anything, so I walk slowly, groping around until I find the bed, and then the hook on the wall for Dracula's robe. My hands are still trembling as I hang up the robe, taking my notebook out of the pocket. I line the slippers up by the bed.

Then I stand there, because I have no idea what to do next.

I try to think. It doesn't work. My mind is spinning around at warp speed like a carousel with no off switch.

So I sit on the bed and press the little button on my watch that makes it glow in the dark. This way, I have a tiny bit of light. Then I open my notebook to a blank page and write across the top:

OPTIONS

1. Go home.

This is the obvious thing to do. Of course, the gates to the park are probably locked, which is exactly what I wanted a few hours ago but which now makes things, well, complicated. I'm not the kind of girl who can hop gates and scale walls. Even if I were, I have no phone, so I can't call anyone to come get me. I have no way of getting to the train station and no money for a train ticket. I'd just end up wandering around the middle of nowhere in the middle of the night, by myself, and that actually seems like a more dangerous situation than the one I'm in.

I cross it out.

2. Turn myself in.

I could walk straight over to the security booth. I could explain everything. Or explain some of it. The more I think about it, the harder that seems. Who runs away to live in an amusement park? And after I confess, what'll happen to me? I doubt you can go to jail when you're twelve, but maybe I'd be sent to juvie.

3. Lie.

I could go to the security booth and, instead of explaining everything, I could make something up. Like, I had a seizure while in the Haunted House, which made me . . . umm, slide under the bed? For a few hours? Or, I could try: I don't know what happened. I was hit over the head with something heavy.

But I just don't think I can pull off a lie that big. That would be a feat for even the best liars, and I am anything but.

I cross out this option, too.

So I'm out of options.

I don't want to waste the battery on my watch, so I turn off its light. Then I turn to Dracula, who is lying there next to me. My eyes have adjusted to the dark, and I can make out the faint outline of his head.

"What do you think, Drac?"

Dracula says nothing.

"Silent treatment, huh? Well, fine. Be that way."

It's dark and my feet are cold. I figure that while I'm deciding what to do, I can at least warm up. So I burrow under the covers. It's surprisingly cozy. I'm wondering if they ever wash these sheets and I think probably not, and then I think what about bedbugs, but honestly, I'm so tired I don't even care.

I was wide-awake a few minutes ago, but now it's totally dark and totally quiet and so warm, and my eyelids are feeling really heavy, like they weigh a hundred pounds. I'm trying to think of a plan, and I'm wondering why would Boy Wonder still be in Foreverland and how long has he been here, and my lids are just so unbelievably heavy, so I think maybe I'll close them just for a second . . .

CHAPTER 14

I have a dream, which starts off wonderful.

I'm bundled up nice and snug in Gwen's hand-me-down sleeping bag covered with Disney princesses—the one I always used to take to slumber parties.

The only part of me sticking out of the sleeping bag is my head. I turn my face to the side and I see my dad, who is zipped up in his sleeping bag next to me. Then I look up, and I see an enormous blue whale. *The* enormous blue whale. We are in the Museum of Natural History, in the marine-life room.

At first, it seems like a memory and not a dream. This really happened. When I was ten, my dad took me to a museum sleepover, and we rolled out our sleeping bags under the blue whale and stayed up late watching movies. It was the most fun ever. It was so much fun that I was almost sorry while it was happening because I knew how disappointed I was going to be when it was over.

My dream starts off with this memory, and I'm feeling really happy. But then a cold dread sinks in, like it's seeping right through my skin, into my bones. Something's wrong—really wrong. I hear this snapping sound coming from above, so I look up and I see the enormous blue whale is swaying. The thick strings that hold it in place are breaking. It's coming loose. I try to scramble to my feet, but I can't move. I try to yell, but I have no voice.

As I watch, the whale starts to swing. It's dangling by a string, just one string. I squeeze my eyes shut tight. When I open them, I'm staring at a vampire face.

For a few seconds, I think I am still having a nightmare. But then it all comes back to me.

The suitcase by the door.

Me on the train.

My backpack gone.

Sleeping in the Haunted House . . .

That's when I hear a knock at the door. The knock wakes me all the way up. I have no idea what time it is, but I know it's morning because I see bright sunlight leaking in around the sides of the thick curtains.

In seconds, I'm out of the bed, pulling the covers up, fast, behind me. I'm almost at the back door when I remember that I'm not wearing any shoes. I sprint back to the bed and fish around underneath for my sandals. It's a good thing, because while I'm doing that, I see my notebook, which must've fallen on the floor while I slept.

I make a terrible criminal, I think as I run,

barefoot, carrying the sandals and notebook, out the back door.

I dart behind the nearest bush and check my watch.

8:06.

I crane my head to the side and squint through the sunlight to see who was knocking. It is now occurring to me that it's sort of a weird thing for someone to do. I mean, it's not a real house or anything. Nobody lives there.

I can make out someone at the front door, but with the glare and the bush in the way, it's hard to see who it is. What I can see is that whoever it is doesn't walk *into* the Haunted House. They walk *away* from it.

And, actually, they're not walking at all. They are cartwheeling.

I know it must be Jaime.

What I don't know is, well, everything else.

I don't have time to figure it out at this exact moment, though, because I hear the sound of voices talking, and through the bushes, I can see a security golf cart zipping down a path nearby. There are a whole bunch of things I have to do all at once:

1. Put on shoes.
2. Hide.
3. Pee.

And I mean, like, wow, do I have to go. I know there's a restroom just a few feet away, so that's where I go, jamming my feet into my sandals on the way.

I'm finished and washing my hands when the door swings open.

A short woman wearing a Foreverland staff T-shirt walks in. She's pushing a cleaning cart loaded with toilet paper and paper towels, and it takes her a second to see me. When she does, she jumps and makes a strangled screaming sound. I do the same thing.

Then she starts laughing.

"Honey, you scared me half to death," she says, chuckling. "They opened up Magic Hour already? Shoot, I must be late."

I blink at her, not wanting to risk opening my mouth. She is really short and stout. She reminds me of the little teapot.

"Honey, this part of the park's not open yet," she says, like she's really sorry about that. "Not for another hour. But Sky City's open, and there's all kinds of stuff by the entrance."

"Uh-huh," I say.

"Go get your money's worth."

"Uh-huh," I repeat, walking out of the bathroom, fast.

I'm panting as I head in the direction of the entrance. This part of the park's still deserted, and

I feel exposed, like a security guard is going to spot me any second. So I follow the sounds of kids laughing. I need to get lost in the crowd again.

Magic Hour, I think, and I can't help giggling.

Magic Hour costs extra, and it allows you to get into Foreverland an hour early, before the park officially opens, so you don't have to wait in such long lines. I've always wanted to try it.

The gates are just now opening, and the first few people are walking through the turnstiles. There are a bunch of Magic Hour tables set up with special activities, like balloon animals and glitter tattoos and face painting. The Bored King of Foreverland, from the parade last night, is there by the entrance, holding a stack of maps. His long hair is unbrushed and his eyes are half-closed, like he's still not awake yet. He hands me a map and mumbles, "Havamagicaday."

While I'm looking at the map, someone says, "Good mornin', sunshine! What's it gonna be?"

I look over and see one of the face painters is talking to me. She is wearing a ton of makeup, all neon colors, and she has her hair in two high pigtails that have silver streamers in them. It looks like she has two cheerleader pom-poms growing out of her head.

"Princess? Butterfly? Pirate?" she asks, waving me into her empty seat.

Before I even know what's happening, she's

sweeping her brush across my forehead and telling me she'll surprise me with a look I'll love. I'm way too old for face painting, and I'm not optimistic about the surprise, but I keep quiet.

This sort of thing happens to me all the time because:

Fun fact: I'm a human pinball.

I don't say yes and I don't say no, so I just get sucked into doing things, just like I'm a pinball getting bopped around a machine.

The face painter's brush is darting and swirling in the different-colored paints and then sweeping and curving across my cheeks and nose, and before I know it, she's saying "Voilà!" and handing me a mirror.

I can't even recognize my own reflection. My eyes are electric blue, staring out from a sea of glittery purple-and-pink swirls.

"Who am I?" I ask. because I honestly don't have a clue.

"A fairy," she replies. "You're not too old for that, are you? Kids these days grow up so fast; I never know."

"No, I'm not too old," I say, and I realize, as I say it, that's it's true. I am really digging the look. "Thanks."

"Have a magical day," she tells me. Which, I know by now, is my cue to move along.

CHAPTER 15

I should probably try to get my backpack and figure out a plan for how to get home. After my close call with the Captain last night, it's pretty obvious that I won't be living at the park. I know my joyride's just about over. It was a total miracle that I didn't get caught already, and I'm not lucky enough to pull it off a second time. Plus, my parents must be freaking out. The note I left will let them know I haven't been abducted by aliens or anything, but still, they must be worried.

So, like it or not, I guess I'm going home. As soon as I can figure out how to get my backpack. Which is high on my list of things to do. But I'm walking right by Sky Seats, one of my favorite rides in the park, and there is no line at all. Really, it would be dumb not to ride it.

I shove my notebook into one of the cubbies for personal belongings, and then I walk onto the ride. It's nothing special or anything—your basic carnival fare, just a bunch of plastic seats that fly out to the side when the ride begins to spin. But a classic is a classic for a reason.

I sit in one of the blue plastic chairs and slide the little metal bar down to fit over my lap. A big group files in, all wearing the same purple T-shirts. On the back, the shirts read ARTS AND SCIENCE GIRLS BASKETBALL.

Right away, I think of Priya.

Priya goes to Arts and Science. Or she did the last time I talked to her, which was almost a year ago. We graduated elementary school and we were inseparable, but then she went to sleepaway camp for a month, so we couldn't talk. Priya wanted me to go with her. She said we could be bunkmates. My mom loved the idea, of course. She kept saying it would be a "transformative experience," which was annoying but also kind of a cool thing to imagine. I wanted to go, I really did, but come on . . . a cabin in the woods? For a month? I get creeped out if I go too deep into Central Park. I wanted to go. I just couldn't.

Priya got back from camp at the end of August, and then there was tons to do to get ready for middle school. She went to Arts and Science, and I went to Whitman. I texted her a bunch and she texted back sometimes, but she seemed distracted and, I don't know, distant. Polite. Just not super interested. So I stopped texting. And that was almost a year ago.

Even under normal circumstances, I wouldn't want to run into Priya, because it would be super awkward. But right now, I *really* don't want to run into Priya, because it would make this mess even messier. My parents probably called Priya last night to see if she knew where I was, which is really embarrassing but also, honestly, a little satisfying. It wouldn't be the worst thing for Priya to wonder for a second how I'm doing. I'm not mad at her or anything, and it's not really her fault that we're not friends anymore, but it's also not *not* her fault, either.

Still, it would be a case of colossally bad timing to run into her right now. I consider unstrapping myself and running off the ride, but I think that will probably attract more attention than staying put. I am the Invisible Girl, after all. Nobody's even looking in my direction.

Plus, Priya would never join the basketball team. Not even the new-and-improved Priya I see posting online. A makeover can do a lot of things, but it can't make you coordinated and cure your asthma.

I try to eavesdrop on the Arts and Science girls' conversation in case someone mentions Priya, but they're too far away and besides, the ride is already starting. Within a few seconds, the girls melt into a blur and I'm not thinking about anything, just gripping the bar and laughing.

I ride again, and again, and then I notice there's no line for the Starship, either, so I ride that, too, and then I get on Pirate's Cove, because, you know, you shouldn't look a gift horse in the mouth or whatever. By the time the Pirate's Cove ship pulls up to the exit platform, my stomach is rumbling too loudly to ignore. So I head to the Pirate's Cove cubbies to collect my notebook.

I notice right away that something's weird.

When I put the notebook in the cubby, my pen was resting on top of the book, but now it's wedged between the pages.

I open the book to where the pen is stuck in. The page has been folded in a complicated way, to make a cool hexagon shape.

Origami.

I unfold the page and read the note.

The handwriting is absolutely terrible. You could call it chicken scrawl, but chickens would be offended. It takes me a while to even figure out what it says, but then I get it:

meet me at the ferris wheel in an hour.

I know two things right away:

1. The note is from Jaime.
2. I'm going to meet him.

And that's it. Those are two sure things bobbing like buoys in a huge ocean of stuff I don't know. Like:

1. What is the deal with this guy? Like, seriously?
2. When are we supposed to meet? I mean,

he didn't include a time stamp, and I'm not sure when he wrote the note.

3. What, when, and how am I going to eat?

Because I am starving. Ravenous. I didn't eat much yesterday, and half of what I ate, I choked on. I'm so hungry I can't think of anything else. I see a kid passing by with a soft pretzel, and my mouth literally starts to water.

I need to eat, which means I need money, which means I need my backpack.

So, I'll:

1. Get my backpack.
2. Get food.
3. Go to the Ferris wheel.
4. Go home.

A quick look at a map tells me that "Valuables Lost and Found" is located in the security booth near the Majestic Theater. That's got to be where my backpack is. I can't help but worry about running into the Captain at security, but I tell myself to calm down. I tell myself that things always seem scarier at night. Especially when you are hiding in an empty Haunted House. I'll just explain that I left my backpack in the Haunted House yesterday and came back to the park today to get it. It's totally reasonable.

So I head over to the security booth. It's almost ten now, so Magic Hour's been over for a while. There's already a line at the Catapult and Shooting Star, and at Sky Seats, too. Not at security, though.

The booth looks cheerful, with a sign in front that reads NEED HELP? JUST ASK! written in the same golden script as everything else in the park. The man sitting behind the glass window is cheerful-looking, too. He's got thin brown hair, thick glasses, and a round, bowl-full-of-jelly belly that makes him look like Santa Claus.

When I walk over, he doesn't notice me for a few seconds, because he's concentrating on some kind of game on his phone. I can't tell what game it is, but it has lots of loud, annoying sound effects.

I stand there for a while waiting for the guy to notice me, but he just jabs at the phone with his finger, like his life depends on it.

Finally, I say, "Hello?"

He jumps up in surprise, and then shoves his phone into a drawer and looks up at me.

"Oh, hi there. Hello, didn't see you . . . There was—" He clears his throat, and his voice gets deep and serious. "I was just taking care of something, um, urgent."

He waits for me to say something, but I have no idea what to say. His voice sounds sort of familiar, which bugs me because I have definitely never met him before. I'd remember someone this strange.

"Okay," I say.

He seems very relieved.

"O-*kay*!" he says, smiling. "So, young lady, what can I do for you?"

"I, umm, I lost my backpack?"

"Well, you've come to the right place! We've got a whole bunch of those. Does this backpack of yours have any identifying characteristics? Moles? Birthmarks? Tattoos?"

This cracks him up—like, *really* cracks him up. Way more than it should. Then, in the middle of his laughing fit, he turns suddenly serious and says, "I hope I didn't offend, young lady. There is absolutely nothing wrong with birthmarks or moles or tattoos. I have many of them myself. Moles. Not tattoos. I have a thing about needles—"

I am full-on staring at him. This guy works in security? It's no wonder no one found me last night.

He interrupts himself: "Yes? What does your backpack look like?"

"It's yellow? It has a patch on it that says 'CAMP CLOVER' and a rabbit foot hanging off the top?"

The guy's eyes light up like I said something really, really interesting. "A rabbit foot."

"Uh-huh."

My stomach, which was rumbling from hunger, starts to churn with nerves. Because the guy who, I'll admit, is weird to begin with, is acting super weird now. Not just weird—suspicious.

"Okay, great. That's *great*. No problem. I'll go get it. I mean, I'll *check* and I will *see* if we have it—which we might. We might not. I can't make any promises."

He is still talking nervously as he walks through a door, out of the small front area, into another part of the booth.

I have a very bad feeling about this. But I have a bad feeling about stuff on a regular basis. If I bolted every time I had a bad feeling, I'd constantly be running. So I don't leave, even though I want to.

Instead, I look around the booth. There are a bunch of bobblehead characters from Disney movies, an open box of doughnuts, and a nameplate.

STEVEN SCHMIDT, it reads.

It takes me a minute to register the name. Which means I figure out who he is at the same exact moment he walks back into the room, holding my backpack. I match his voice to the voice on the other end of the walkie-talkie last night just as he lifts one off his belt and says, "Base to Captain. Do you copy?"

I know two things at once.

1. I'm not getting my backpack.
2. Not having my backpack is the least of my problems.

CHAPTER 16

I run.

I run without having any idea where I'm going. I run at top speed until I crash into a couple holding hands who yell at me to watch where I'm going.

Then I stop for a split second to pick up my notebook, which has fallen to the ground, and I take this opportunity to glance behind me. There's no one following me. I am panting so hard, my lungs burn. So I stand there for a second to catch my breath, and that's when I realize I'm just a few steps away from the Ferris wheel, aka the Wheel of Magic.

It occurs to me that maybe the safest place I can be right now is many, many feet up in the air. I speed-walk over to the Wheel of Magic entrance. I have no idea where I am supposed to meet Jaime or when, really, so I decide to just get on. I have a feeling he'll be able to find me.

The line's short, and in just a few minutes, I'm at the front.

"You wanna rock?" the ride operator asks, and I'm about to say "No" as clearly as I can, because even though I like the Ferris wheel just fine, I really do not like the rocking cars.

I can't possibly stress this enough.

Rocking cars and I go together like peanut butter and someone who is really allergic to peanut butter.

We do not go together at all. We should be kept far, far apart.

Before I can tell her that, though, someone is grabbing my hand and pulling me onto the car that's waiting in front of me. I'm so surprised, I don't have time to protest, and I find myself sitting opposite Boy Wonder as the door to the car clangs shut.

"Nice face," he says, grinning.

I'm totally confused because "Nice face" is not how you usually start a conversation with *anyone*, especially someone you hardly know.

Then I remember that I had my face painted, and it makes more sense.

While I am trying to figure out how you respond to "Nice face," Jaime says, "You're right on time."

I am speechless. It's not that I don't have anything to say. It's that I have too much. A huge swarm of questions is buzzing around in my brain. I don't know where to start.

How can I be right on time when you never said when to meet?

Also, just a minor question: WHAT DO YOU WANT?

And, while we're on the subject, are you the dangerous kind of weird or the harmless kind?

But there's only one question that I really need an answer to immediately:

"Is this a rocking car?" I blurt out. "I can't go on those."

The question gets answered before he has a chance to reply. The Ferris wheel lurches forward, and it is immediately clear what kind of car we're in.

"Oh no," I whimper. "Oh no, no, no. I can't. I can't be on here."

My heart is racing, and everything sounds muffled like I'm under a waterfall.

As we're lifted higher in the air, our car rocks back and forth. Except that *rocking* is not the right word for it. Rocking is what you do to a baby when you're trying to lull it to sleep. Rocking is gentle.

Our car is swinging like a pendulum.

My arms fly out to the sides and I press them there, so I'm sort of braced. I stick my fingers through the grating on the windows, and I clench as tight as I can. My heart is pounding so fast that I can't even make out a beat anymore, just a roar of *THUMPTHUMPTHUMPTHUMPTHUMP*.

Jaime's not smiling anymore. He looks worried. His dark eyebrows are furrowed together, and his big eyes get even bigger.

"Are you okay?"

I shake my head, but with the car swinging it's too much shaking, and I feel a big wave of nausea hit me. So I close my eyes and drop my head.

"I have to get off. Tell them. Make them stop it."

"I'm sorry. For real. I didn't know you were scared," I hear him say. "But there's only one way off this thing, and that's to go around."

He's right, of course. What goes up must come down. Unless you're talking about my last meal. In that case, what goes down must come up. I'm suddenly really glad I haven't eaten anything all morning.

I'm also suddenly furious. Being furious actually makes me feel less scared, so I go with it.

"This is totally your fault!" I snap open my eyes. "I didn't want to go in a rocking car! You didn't even give me a chance to choose! What's wrong with you?"

"Now, *that's* the million-dollar question. Many have tried to figure it out, but all have failed."

"It's *not* funny," I growl. "You're, like, a sociopath."

"Possible," he says, smiling. "Of course, I'm not the one sleeping in a haunted house."

At that moment, the Ferris wheel freezes.

"Huh?" I ask.

"That's why I thought you'd be cool with the rocking car," he says. "You're sleeping in a haunted

96

house, and that's hard-core. You got guts. So I just figured, you know, nothing scares you."

"I'm not . . . I mean, I don't know what you're talking about?"

He laughs again.

"If that's your act for the Captain, it needs a lot of work," he says. "I know you were in the Haunted House. I saw you."

"Hold on," I say. Because we've been stopped long enough that our car isn't rocking anymore, so I'm not panicking. Even though my brain is running in circles and jumping up like a frisky puppy, I've at least got ahold of the leash now. I can form sentences. It suddenly occurs to me that the upside of us being trapped in this car is that he can't just vanish into thin air with no warning. Which means I can finally get some answers to my questions.

"We need to talk," I tell him. "I have questions."

"Shoot," he says.

"Okay, well, so . . . if you saw me at the Haunted House after closing, then you obviously spent the night here, too."

Jaime says nothing, just raises his eyebrows at me. "I'm waiting for the question."

I sigh heavily, then say, "Did you sleep here last night? Have you been here a while? What's your deal?"

Jaime starts cracking the knuckles on his right

hand, tugging on each finger in a way that sets my teeth on edge.

"I'm crashing here for a bit," he says. "Like you. Only, I'm not as hard-core as you. No way I could sleep in the Haunted House with the skeletons. I mean, don't get me wrong. It's perfect. What'd you do? Take the last tour, then hide somewhere when they turned the lights out?"

I don't want to be flattered, but I can't help it. I am. "Yeah, under the bed."

He whistles.

"Nice."

It's starting to freak me out that the Ferris wheel isn't moving. I mean, I love that it isn't moving, but is it normal? What if the ride's broken? We're not at the tip-top of the wheel, but we're close, and I have no idea how they would get us down. Crane? Helicopter?

Jaime must notice that I look worried, because he scooches over to the side of the car and peers down below. This shifts our balance, and we start rocking again.

"Can you—can you not?"

"Sorry," he says, sliding back, which makes the car rock even more.

"It's a meltdown. That little girl doesn't want to get on the Ferris wheel, doesn't want to get out of the way. We might be a while."

"So you're crashing here 'for a bit'? Which means . . . what, exactly? A few days?"

"I've been here a while." He says it like he's being modest, but I can tell he's really proud of himself. "Almost long enough to wear out my welcome. But I got security off my scent . . . until the Captain found your backpack. Now he's all revved up again."

"You know about my backpack?"

"Listen, here's the deal," Jaime says. "I know everything that goes on here. Everything."

I roll my eyes at him.

"For real," he says. "But the truth is, not much goes on. After a while, this place gets so boring."

I hear a shriek from down below and a kid's voice yelling, "No, no, NO! I don't WANNA move! YOU CAN'T MAKE ME!"

"What did I tell you?" Jaime says. "It happens every day. That's the thing. I've been here long enough that nothing surprising ever happens. I have seen it all. I've seen two different people propose on the Catapult."

"Seriously?"

He nods.

"Yeah, and they *both* dropped the rings and never found them. Serves them right for being stupid."

I laugh in spite of myself.

"I have seen forty-seven people throw up—most of them on Vertigo Vortex. I've seen six people lose their bathing suits in Tsunami Falls. I helped ten different lost boys find their parents in Tot Town. And

I've been on the Shooting Star, well, I've been on so many times, I lost count. So, I'm sort of . . . over it."

"So why don't you just go home? Aren't your parents looking for you?"

He laughs this bitter, hollow laugh and says, "No, they're not."

Then he peers back down at the kid having a tantrum.

"Uh-oh." He laughs. "She's got ahold of the railing. When they get ahold of the railing, it's serious. The parents try to pry their fingers off, but it's not as easy as it looks."

"Okay, so, not to be rude, but what do you want from me?"

He looks at me with this confused expression, like he doesn't understand.

"What do you mean?"

"I mean, why are you, like, following me around and writing in my notebook—which, by the way, is a total invasion of privacy. What do you want?"

His eyes look really sad all of a sudden.

Then he shrugs. "I just wanna hang out. I haven't had a conversation in . . . a long time. You can't talk to the guests—you know that, right? If you do, people get suspicious. That's how the Captain almost caught me the last time."

There is a clanging sound from down below, and then the Ferris wheel lurches back on.

We go up and up, and then we are at the top

of the wheel. The whole park is so very small; all the people look like little dollhouse people. Even though I am 98 percent terrified, I am 2 percent amazed by how beautiful it is.

As I am busy taking deep breaths, I hear Jaime say, "Oh man. Check out the security booth."

It takes me a minute to find the booth, but when I do, I gasp a little. The booth is surrounded by security guards and the little golf carts they ride around on. It looks like they're having a security convention down there.

Jaime whistles. "Somebody caught their attention. And it wasn't me this time."

"Oh no."

"What'd you do? Ask for your backpack or something?" Jaime's laughing.

The car is rocking like crazy, and I can't think straight. Everything's a mess. All I want to do is get off this Ferris wheel.

"I gotta get off this thing," I say, and then I yell down, "Hey! Hello!!"

"I'm not trying to tell you what to do," Jaime says, "but you probably don't want to make a big scene. You know, with security looking for you already."

He's right, of course.

"Just relax," he says. "It'll be over soon."

I sit back on the ride but I do not relax.

"So," he says, "what do you wanna go on next?"

"I'm not going on anything next," I snap. "There are about a hundred people looking for me. I have to get to the train station and go home—even though it's the last place I want to be, and also, I have no idea how to get there, since I have no money, since all my money and my train ticket are in that stupid backpack."

"You want your backpack?" he says. "I can get it, no problem."

I am skeptical and I must be showing it.

"What? You don't believe me?"

On the one hand, I do believe him because he's the same person that saved me from a hot dog and levitated on the Starship and gave me a handy wake-up call before the park opened this morning.

On the other hand, the only thing I really know about him is that he is absolutely and completely unpredictable. Which doesn't inspire a ton of confidence.

"No, it's fine. I'll just . . . I'll figure it out," I tell him.

The Wheel of Magic is slowing down now, and our car has almost reached the ground.

"I'll get the backpack for you, I promise," he says, sliding forward in his seat. "All right? Don't leave the park yet."

"No, really—"

"Just gimme an hour. And while you wait, wash

your face. No one'll recognize you if you wash the face paint off. Solid idea, the face paint."

I do not tell him the face paint was an accident and not some genius master plan to disguise myself. I don't say anything, because the ride operator is opening the door to our car and I'm leaping out.

He walks alongside me for a second. "I'll meet you in an hour, in Games. I'll have your backpack, I promise."

"I don't—" I start to say, but he doesn't hear me, because he's already sprinting away in the direction of the security booth.

I'm back on the ground but my head's still spinning.

Boy Wonder has a plan.

And I'm not sure, but I think I have a partner in crime.

CHAPTER 17

I take Jaime's suggestion, mostly because I don't have any other ideas. I find the nearest bathroom, which is in Tot Town, and I scrub my face clean. I have to use a ton of paper towels and soap, but finally the face paint comes off.

After that, I'm not sure what to do. The reasonable thing, I know, is to find a phone, call my parents, and explain everything. They probably both stayed home from work today, and Gwen probably missed swim practice, too. I remember the way my mother's voice used to sound calling my name as I hid in the back of the coat closet—the desperation that made her voice high and thin. I realize that while I was sleeping in the Haunted House, they were probably wide-awake, searching my room for clues about where I went, reading and rereading my mysterious acrostic. They probably didn't sleep all night. I wonder if my mother cried. She never cries.

The more I think about this, the heavier my body feels, because I know this adventure has gone on long enough. I really should get home soon.

And then the image of the red suitcase pops back into my mind, and it's like I've been touched by an electric spark, I feel so suddenly hot and hurt. This mess isn't my fault. It's theirs.

This makes me feel a little less guilty about my parents waiting, worried, by the phone, huddled on the couch together. Together.

It occurs to me that as long as I'm gone, my parents will be stuck together. And maybe if they're stuck together long enough . . .

I am fully aware this is a dumb idea.

But I'm on a dumb-idea roll. And also, stranger things have happened. And also, I don't want to call them. I don't want them to swoop to the rescue. I want to walk through the front door when I decide I'm good and ready. And I can do that, as soon as I get my wallet back.

So, really, I just need to stay put and wait for Jaime to get my backpack.

I decide not to wander around the park while I'm waiting. I want to keep a low profile until I know the coast is clear. So I walk out of the bathroom and sit down at the nearest table in the Tot Town food court. I take out my notebook.

I'm trying to think of a good acrostic to write when I hear a man's voice talking to me.

"Mind if we share with you?"

It's a dad, with his wife and two little boys—all of them in matching Foreverland sun visors.

They are holding plastic trays heaped with fried food—burgers, corn dogs, and fries, oh my!—and I think the dad is asking if they can share their food with me.

"Yes! Thank you!" I exclaim.

The mom and dad give me confused looks, and then I realize that, of course, they want to share my table, not their food. It's after eleven, so it's really crowded and there are no other free tables.

I die of embarrassment.

Fun fact: Dying of embarrassment does not get easier with practice.

The family settles in at the other end of my table. I can't help staring at their food. There is so much of it, and it smells so, so good. I am tantalized by the smell of sweet ketchup and greasy burgers and—most irresistible of all—freshly fried potatoes. My mouth gets all watery.

I watch the littlest boy take a big bite of his burger. His teeth sink into the bun, and juicy morsels of ketchup and onions and lettuce fall out onto his plate. It's pure torture to watch. I force myself to look down at my notebook. I scribble:

Bonanza of

Unbelievably

Ridiculously

Good flavors that I am dying to

Eat

Right now.

Don't think about burgers, I tell myself. *Or crispy, juicy chicken tenders or glistening piles of chocolate soft serve covered in crunchy chocolate sprinkles. And definitely do not think about french fries.*

My stomach is rumbling so loudly, it's like a beast yelling *FEED ME FEED ME FEED ME*.

Maybe it's the way I stared at the little boy like I was going to eat him, or maybe it was the alien noises coming from my stomach, but Matching Visor Family leaves. They stand up and walk away, leaving their trays of garbage behind.

If my mom were here, this would make her so mad.

"It's just common courtesy," she'd say. "Bus your tray."

It's weird because I find myself thinking this, too, like my mom's voice is possessing me. Because I am a neat freak like her, I can't stand to see garbage cluttering the table, and I'm about to toss the stuff in the trash when I realize: This isn't trash. It's treasure.

The older brother left a whole pile of fries on his plate, and if I just lift the crumpled napkin off the dish, I can eat them. If I can get over the tremendous gross factor.

Fun fact: I don't share food. Why not just lick a toilet seat?

My parents and Gwen tease me about it. They call me a germophobe. And maybe I am. But it's not irrational or anything. In fact, what's actually irrational is to share food with people. Stop to consider how many illnesses are spread through saliva: strep; swine flu; regular flu; hepatitis; pertussis; hand, foot and mouth disease; typhoid . . . there are too many to list.

"I'm pretty sure I don't have typhoid," Gwen would say, when I'd refuse to taste her smoothie.

"Nobody thinks they have typhoid until they do," I'd reply. "That's the whole point."

My germ thing was a problem in school last winter. Kids would constantly cough, and nobody—*nobody*—would cough into their elbow. I tried not to make a big deal about it, but I guess I would flinch whenever someone coughed near me.

One day Greta, who sat next to me in math, noticed I was flinching. That's when she got the most *hilarious* idea to intentionally cough right in my face. She must've told her crony drones about it, because by the end of the day, there was a whole bunch of them hacking directly in my face and smirking like Disney villains or something. That delightful fun lasted all winter. I got strep and a stomach bug, and I blame Greta and her evil friends for both.

So I have a germ thing.

But I also have a need-to-eat thing. And right now, that's stronger.

Besides, I tell myself, *that family looked very healthy. I didn't hear a single sneeze.*

I pick up a long, crispy french fry and scrutinize it for signs of typhoid. I'm not entirely sure what typhoid looks like on a french fry, but this one looks pretty clean. And oily. And salty. And delicious.

I shove the fry in my mouth. It tastes even better than I'd imagined. As soon as I eat the first one, I'm all in. In about two minutes, I've cleared off what was left on the plate and also what was on the other plates, too, which wasn't much. I even go so far as to devour the rogue fries that fell on the tray. Then I push the tray across the table, as if I didn't just scavenge for lunch from the garbage.

The trouble is, eating has only made me hungrier. It's like the few fries in my stomach have energized the beast in there. Now he's roaring, *MORE MORE MORE OR YOU'LL BE SORRY.*

I look around for any other trays with leftovers. What I find, instead, is Jaime. He's standing right next to me.

He does not have my backpack.

He does have a whole bunch of other stuff.

His arms are overflowing with clothes and accessories, which he dumps onto the table in front of me.

"Wasn't I supposed to meet you in Games?" I ask. "In"—I check my watch—"fifteen minutes?"

He shrugs.

"And hey, where's my backpack?"

"I'm working on it."

He puts an extra-large foam fountain beverage cup right in front of me. I can hear the ice cubes clinking around.

"For you," he says.

I don't know what's in there, but I'm so thirsty, I take a huge slurp.

Icy-cold root beer. Perfect.

Jaime reaches into the big pocket of his cargo shorts and pulls out a burger-shaped bundle, wrapped in foil with the Foreverland logo on it.

It looks like a burger.

It smells like a burger.

I unwrap the foil and, sure enough, it is a burger. Correction: a double cheeseburger.

"First step in the plan," says Jaime. "Fortify."

But I'm already cramming as much of the burger into my mouth as will fit. Globs of ketchup and mustard and hamburger juice slide down my arm, but I don't mind.

He places another foil bundle in front of himself and starts eating, too. I'm almost done with my burger by the time he takes his first bite.

"Take it easy, cowgirl," says Jaime. "Don't forget what happened with the hot dog yesterday. I can't make it a habit, saving your life."

"You didn't save my life," I say. Or try to say. My mouth is full of cow.

"Wanna bet?"

"I do," I reply. "I do want to bet. But I can't. I have no money. That's in my backpack. Which you said you'd get for me."

His mouth breaks into an enormous smile.

"All right, all right, fine," he says. "I'll tell you the plan."

"Proceed."

"First step, fortify." He takes another bite of burger.

"We covered that," I say. "Hey, by the way, where'd you get the food? Do you have money?"

"I don't need money."

I put what's left of my burger—which is hardly anything—down on the foil.

"Did you steal this? I don't want stolen burgers."

He grabs the cup and takes a big sip of root beer. This makes my skin crawl but I try not to show it.

"Relax, would you? I didn't steal anything. I've got friends in high places. Or friends in a food court, at least. You *could* say thank you."

"Thank you," I say as I inhale the rest of the burger.

"So, second step." He grins. "Makeover."

"Huh?"

"Schmidt got a good look at you, right? The face paint helped, but it's not enough. We need to get all witness-protection program with you."

He pushes the pile of clothes toward me.

"Lucky for you, people lose all sorts of stuff in this place."

"You claimed all this from the Lost and Found? From Schmidt?"

He slurps more root beer and shakes his head.

"They only lock up valuables like phones and wallets and bags and stuff. They just throw this junk in the regular Lost and Found, which is basically a huge dumpster. No one ever claims this stuff."

I pick up one of the pieces of clothing, pinching it between my thumb and middle finger because it looks really dirty. It's a men's Hawaiian shirt with blue and white flowers all over it.

"*This* is going to help me blend in?"

"Well, maybe not that one," he says, chewing a bite of burger. "But I brought you a bunch of options."

There are pink Bermuda shorts, a striped sundress, camo pants, a sequined red halter top, and a bright yellow T-shirt that has huge black letters that read I ❤ MARMOSETS.

I hold this one up and look at him.

"Options? You call these options?"

"Okay, not that one, either."

"I'm not going to wear any of these. Not only

are they, seriously, the *most* conspicuous clothes I have *ever* seen, they are one hundred percent crawling with lice and scabies and who knows what else."

"What's scabies?"

"It's like lice but for your whole body."

"Nasty."

"Exactly."

"You can see scabies?" he asks.

"No, I can't *see* them."

"So you don't know this stuff has them, then. It's a guess?"

"A hypothesis."

"Which is a guess."

"Sure."

He pops the last bite of burger into his mouth and crumples the foil wrapper into a tiny ball, then tosses it into the trash. The can is at least ten feet away, but he gets it in.

"So what?" he asks.

"What do you mean, 'So what?'"

He slurps the drink again. Finishes it, actually. I can hear the sound of ice getting sucked dry.

"So what if the clothes have rabies?"

"Scabies."

"Scabies, whatever. Big deal. Who cares?"

"I care."

He is picking through the clothes, looking for something.

"They're not deadly, right? You will survive?"

"I guess."

"So who cares?"

I don't know how to respond to this. It's not like any conversation I've ever had. It's like talking to the Cheshire Cat.

He tosses something at me. It's a gray-and-blue soccer jersey, with the words EASTSIDE SOCCER and the number nine on the back.

Then he tosses something else my way. Overall shorts.

"Okay, I have a lot to say here," I start. "But my first question is: Who forgets their overalls at an amusement park? Like, how exactly does that happen?"

Jaime bursts out laughing. Just like his smile, his laugh is Extra Strength. Totally contagious.

He tosses me a pair of pink sunglasses with butterflies on the sides.

"You can't go full incognito without shades."

Then he slides a pair over his own eyes. The lenses are mirrored, just like the Captain's, and I see my reflection in them. My brows are furrowed and I look suspicious.

Is this what I always look like? I think.

Because if it is, then no wonder I have no friends. This look basically screams, *I am thoroughly opposed to fun! Go away!*

Jaime stands up, gathers all the rest of the clothes on the table, and stuffs them into the garbage.

"What are you doing?" I ask. "That stuff belongs to people!"

But he's already walking away. "*Vámonos!*" he calls over his shoulder. "*El tiempo no espera a ningún hombre.*"

I grab my notebook and the clothing picks and rush after him. "What does that mean?"

"Let's go!" he calls over his shoulder. "Time waits for no man!"

CHAPTER 18

I have to sprint to catch up with Jaime. He walks fast. Really fast. I don't know how he can walk so fast and not be running.

"You speak Spanish?" I ask him.

"Sure," he says. "Doesn't everyone?"

"No," I say, panting. "Not everyone. I mean, I don't."

"Huh," he says. "What do you speak?"

"Latin."

"For real?"

I nod. "I mean, I'm not fluent or whatever. I take it at school."

He lunges forward and then he's walking again, only now on his hands.

"Does anybody even speak Latin anymore?" he says. While walking on his hands. Like this is a perfectly normal way to carry on a conversation.

"Not really," I admit. "But speaking isn't the only way to communicate. It's a *written* language. Lots of books are written in Latin."

He doesn't say anything, and I figure he's not listening. Since he's walking on his hands and all.

Then he sticks his feet on the ground and jumps upright again.

"You would rather read a book in a dead language than talk to someone?"

I shrug. "Depends on the book."

We're walking through Tot Town, past the flying-elephant ride and the one my dad calls Baby Hells Angels, because it has tiny motorcycles for toddlers to ride on.

"You need to talk to more interesting people," he says.

"Maybe you need to read more interesting bo—" Before I can finish, Jaime's grabbing my hand and yanking me, hard, to the ground. We're crouching behind a bush next to the big Tot Town Tree House.

I'm about to ask what he's doing when a security cart drives right in front of us, with Schmidt in the driver's seat. We watch the cart get smaller and smaller as it heads toward Magic Mile.

"No time to waste," Jaime says, on the move again.

"Hey, Jaime? Jaime!" I scramble to my feet but still, I'm a few steps behind. I feel like I'm always a few steps behind Jaime—not just when we're walking but when we're talking, too. His mind zips around so fast, it's impossible to keep up.

I have a ton of questions. I want to know where his parents are, and how long he plans to stay here, and how he got the free burgers, and where he learned Spanish, and, oh yeah, what are steps three, four, five, and whatever, in this plan to get my backpack back?

But there's never a chance to ask any of these questions, because something new is always happening.

"Jaime!" I pant as I rush after him. "Where are we *going*?"

"We're here," he announces, making a ta-da! gesture. What he's gesturing to is a door, next to a sign that reads FAMILY RESTROOM.

"It's a bathroom," I say.

"A *private* bathroom," he corrects. "Also known as your dressing room."

* * *

I'm already sliding my arms into the too-big soccer jersey when I stop to wonder why I'm following Jaime's instructions. I stop to wonder why, but I do it anyway, stepping into the overall shorts. Jaime's just so sure about everything, and I, well, I'm never really sure about anything. The overalls are a little small, but I can loosen the straps so they fit okay.

Don't think about lice eggs hatching. Don't think about bedbugs crawling on your skin, I tell myself. And, presto! Suddenly, I'm really, really itchy.

I'm scratching my arm as I open the door of the bathroom, holding my old clothes in my other hand.

Jaime pulls off his borrowed sunglasses and hangs them on the neck of his T-shirt.

"Who are you and what have you done with Margaret?" he asks, fake-concerned.

Then he takes the bunched-up clothes out of my hand, walks past me into the bathroom, and shoves them into the garbage.

"Hey!" I exclaim. "You need to stop doing that!"

He looks surprised. "Oh, sorry, I didn't think they were special."

"They're not, like, *special*, but—"

But he's not listening anymore. He's already on to the next thing. I can tell because he's reaching into his cargo shorts pocket again. These are some bottomless pockets. Like clown cars or Mary Poppins's bag of tricks. There is no limit to what they can hold.

This time, he pulls out a big pair of scissors. The kind my mom uses to cut chicken cutlets.

Even though I trust Jaime a lot, for some weird, random reason, that trust has limits. So when he takes a step toward me with the scissors, I do something that surprises both of us. Without thinking, I knock them out of his hand.

I use a block move I learned in this self-defense class my mom made me take last summer. The whole time I was in the class—five Sundays—I thought, *This is so dumb. I am never going to remember this crap when I actually need it.*

And now, I am shocked because I do remember. I mean, my brain doesn't, but my arm does.

I whack Jaime's arm with my arm, and the scissors clatter to the tile floor.

Jaime takes a step back, and I grab the scissors, holding them with the sharp part pointed down. Safety position.

I think Jaime's going to be annoyed or angry or something, but he laughs.

"Hard-core," he says.

"What's the deal with the scissors, Jaime?"

"For the makeover," he says, like he's told me this a hundred times already.

"I've already done your gross makeover."

"Haven't you ever seen an extreme makeover show before?" he asks, genuinely confused. "You need a haircut."

I'm getting used to the feeling I have, the I-have-too-many-questions-and-don't-even-know-where-to-start feeling.

"*You* watch extreme makeover shows?" I ask.

"My grandma loves them."

"Your grandma loves them?" I repeat. It's the first thing he's said about his family.

And then, he's explaining that really, it's best to do the cut with a color change, too, but he couldn't get his hands on any bleach.

"Jaime!" I say. Because sometimes, I feel like he's an untamed horse taking me for a wild ride and I just have to yank on the reins so he'll pause for a second.

"Yeah?"

"Jaime," I start again, more calmly. "You don't give people haircuts without their permission. It's, like, the Golden Rule of Stylists. No surprise attacks."

"Okay, okay, you don't have to cut your hair if you don't want to."

"I didn't say I don't want to."

"Ohhhhhh-kay," he says, with his eyebrows raised. Then he mutters, "Girls are weird."

I turn to face my reflection in the mirror.

Fun fact: I'm not a fan of mirrors.

I try to avoid my reflection when possible. It's not that I think I'm hideous or anything. I think it's so annoying when girls at school call themselves ugly and complain about how they look.

I don't think I'm ugly. I just think I'm plain. Like, more plain than a lukewarm glass of water.

When I look at my reflection, the pale-faced, brown-haired, blank-eyed girl just doesn't feel like me. I'm surprised every time to see my reflection— like, *who is that?*—and then, immediately, a little disappointed—*oh, it's me.*

And that's what I think now.

"Look," Jaime is saying, "it's not a big deal. You can put on a hat, I guess. I just thought—"

And while he is talking, I am pulling my pony-tail taut with my left hand. Then, with my other hand, I lop the whole thing off at the base.

It takes a couple of cuts because the ponytail is pretty thick, but in a few seconds, I am holding my long brown ponytail in my hand.

I don't know what to do with it, so I toss it in the trash. The swinging top of the trash spins around—once, twice, three times.

Jaime is whooping and whistling and starting sentences but not finishing them. "Oh my—are you?—that's—wow."

I half expect to start crying, but the truth is, I don't feel sad at all. In fact, it kind of feels amazing. I laugh out loud. Jaime laughs, too. Then I shake my head out, like models do in shampoo commercials. When I look in the mirror again, my hair's up to my ears. It's scraggly and uneven but, actually, it looks kind of great.

I comb my hair the best I can with my fingers. Then I snip off the longer strands to make it more even. With each cut, I feel more and more hopeful, and light, too. It's like each strand of hair weighs an actual ton, and when I cut it, I'm a whole ton lighter.

"I wasn't going to cut it *that* short," Jaime pipes up. He's standing in the corner, shaking his head in disbelief. "Do you, um, like it?"

"Yeah," I reply, and it's true. "But it's missing something."

I comb a bunch of the hair down in front of my face so it hangs there like a curtain. Then I slide the curtain of hair in between the scissor blades, right at the level of my eyebrows.

Whoosh.

The last ton of weight falls off me. I open my eyes and look in the mirror.

The bangs are shorter than I meant for them to be, higher than my eyebrows, but actually I like them like that. It makes the short bob I gave myself look like a flapper cut. My hair looks darker. My eyes look brighter. Glow-y. Like someone replaced the light bulbs.

My face is like a room where someone just moved all the furniture around. Even though it's the same furniture, it finally fits the room the right way.

In a comic book, the person in the mirror would be bizarro me.

In a soap opera, she'd be my evil twin.

But in real life, there's nothing evil or bizarre about this version of me. Actually, it's just the opposite.

I don't feel incognito. It feels like I've finally taken off the costume I've been wearing for a long, long time.

CHAPTER 19

"What now?" I ask Jaime as he pushes open the door of the bathroom. We walk into the blinding sunshine.

"What do you mean?" He slides his mirrored sunglasses over his ears. I catch a glimpse of my reflection in them, and my new look puts a bounce in my step.

"I mean, what's next in this plan you've cooked up to get my backpack? We've completed the make-over part, right? I mean, you don't have a hot-roller set or a tie-dye kit in your pocket, right?"

Jaime breaks out laughing but doesn't slow down.

"I said I was sorry about the scissors." He pulls a floppy blue bucket hat out of his pocket and tosses it to me. "Put that on and your makeover's done. No way Schmidt will recognize you now."

I give the hat a good shake to get rid of whatever creepy-crawlies might be on it, and then I put it on, along with the pink sunglasses.

"Okay, so what's our move here?" I ask. "If I try to claim the backpack—"

"We're not going to claim it."

"So what, then? We're going to steal it?"

"It's not stealing if it's already yours."

"Okay, Robin Hood. But, I mean, how? What's the plan?"

"You reeeeeeeally like plans, don't you?" He stops in his tracks all of a sudden to look at me. "Hey, what are you doing here, anyway? What's your deal?"

This takes me totally by surprise. He hasn't seemed remotely interested in my story, and suddenly he's burning with curiosity.

Now it's my turn to walk ahead. It's hard to walk fast because the path is really crowded with whining kids and annoyed parents and lots of strollers that take up too much room. So I can't really achieve the speed-walk I'm going for, but I try anyway.

Jaime chases after me.

"C'mon," he says. "You don't seem like the runaway type. So what's the story?"

"I just had a craving for a foot-long frank."

"Yeah, right," he snorts. "I've never seen someone mess up eating a hot dog as bad as you did. Even my grandpa chews his food better. And he has no teeth."

"I chew my food just fine. Usually. Yesterday was an exception. I'm just—I'm not used to hot dogs."

"Yeah, I could tell. But how is that even possible? You been living in a bunker or something?"

Now it's my turn to stop and face him.

"What about you, huh? What are *you* doing here?"

"You first."

"No, you."

"You."

"You."

I cross my arms over my chest. "What are you, five years old?"

"Fine," he says. "Whoever loses the staring contest goes first."

"Sorry, my mistake. You're three."

But it's too late. He's already fixing his big, brown eyes on me. It feels like they are burning a hole in my retinas, like I'm staring directly at the sun.

Fun fact: Eye contact is not my strong suit.

It's another thing my mom constantly nags me about. First, she lectures me about my question voice? And then, she starts up with: "If you want to command respect, you have to look people in the eye. It's a sign of weakness to always be looking at your feet."

Staring at Jaime is so incredibly, unbearably uncomfortable that I look away after about three seconds.

"Are you kidding me?" he shrieks. "You're worse at staring than you are at eating hot dogs."

"You're too kind."

"You lost . . . so tell me why you're here." He starts chanting, like a preschooler. "Tell me! Tell me! Tell me!"

"Does this usually work for you? Annoying people into submission?"

"Pretty much every time." He flashes me a thousand-watt smile.

I start walking again.

"I just like this place. And I'm not a big fan of home right now. My parents are being . . ." It's hard to find the words, so I settle on "Stupid."

"Stupid how?"

I don't say anything.

"C'mon. Margarita."

"Margarita?"

He shrugs. "Just trying it out."

I sigh. "It was the suitcase."

"The suitcase?"

"I woke up yesterday, and I was going to get some cereal and go to this boring computer-programming camp my mom signed me up for, even though I am not into computers, like, at all. The house was empty because my parents had left for work, and my sister was at the pool where she now, apparently, lives. But whatever—the house is always empty. It was just a normal day. And then I saw the suitcase by the door."

Jaime's not saying anything, which is a first for him. The path isn't crowded anymore, so we can walk side by side. For once Jaime's not doing acrobatics or playing with a yo-yo. He's just listening to me, which actually feels really great.

"And the thing is, I love this suitcase. Which is maybe a weird thing to say, but it's cherry red and part of a matching set. They're all different sizes so they fit inside of each other, like those Russian nesting dolls—"

"Ohhhh yeah, those are cool."

"And we've had these suitcases my whole life, and I love them because—I don't know—they remind me of vacations and all the fun stuff. So when I saw the suitcase, all packed, by the door, I was so excited for a second. I thought we were going on a surprise vacation or something. But of course, we weren't going anywhere. My dad was, but not the rest of us."

"He moved out?"

I nod. A lump has formed in my throat and I gulp down. "Last night was his last night living with us. Or it was supposed to be, anyway. We were all going to have one Last Supper—a nice dinner all together, like it was some kind of *going away* party or something."

"That's messed up."

"It is. It is totally messed up." I know I'm talking fast and getting excited, but I don't really care. I can't remember the last time someone let me talk for this long.

"And then after this Last Supper, my dad was going to go to his new apartment. With the suitcase. And that's what got me really angry for some reason—that he was taking that suitcase. I mean, it's part of a matching set. Now the set is going to be *missing* a part. It was just making me furious. So I started kicking the stupid suitcase until it finally fell over."

"You roughed up the suitcase?"

"Yeah. Because I'm so hard-core." I smile. "And when it fell over, I saw this picture underneath it, on the floor. I guess my dad had packed it but it fell out, or maybe he dragged it out of the closet accidentally with the suitcase, but either way, it was lying there on the floor."

The picture is still in my notebook, which I've shoved in my overalls pocket. I take it out and hand it to Jaime. He stops walking to look.

"This is your sister?"

"Yeah. The bright, shining star of the family."

"And you're—what? A black hole? I don't buy that." Jaime looks up at me. "There can be more than one star. The sky's full of them."

"Not in the city," I say.

He laughs. "Well, here we've got plenty to go around."

I wipe the sweat off my forehead. The sun is beating down on us like it's got some kind of vendetta. I think of how I should probably apply sunscreen and then remember it's in my backpack. I'll do it later.

Jaime's looking at the picture again. "Your dad looks nice. He looks funny."

"My dad *is* nice. And funny. And the only one who didn't act like I was an alien life-form. But it doesn't matter now, because he's bailing. Which he promised—flat-out promised—he would never do. So in addition to everything else, he's a liar."

My voice kind of breaks a little, and I'm scared that I'm going to start crying, which would be the worst possible thing that could happen at this moment. I take the picture out of Jaime's hands and stick it back in my notebook.

"Margaret," he says. "That really sucks."

I shrug. "Whatever. It's fine. Half of marriages end in divorce." I start walking down the path again, even though I have no idea where we're headed. I just want to be moving.

"So you saw that picture yesterday and you decided to come to Foreverland?" Jaime asks.

"When you put it that way, it seems random,"

I say. "But the day in this picture, the last time we came here—that was also our last great day together. In the car, we rolled the windows down and sang along to the radio, all of us together. My parents held hands. The whole day was really, just, nice. It was a good memory."

"Yeah," says Jaime. "I get that."

"So I just started throwing stuff in my backpack without even thinking about it, really, and then I was on the train and now I'm here." I glance over at Jaime, whose face is looking kind of saggy and weird. I kick myself for dishing up way too much personal information and making things awkward. I try to lighten the mood.

"And by the way, I don't have that backpack anymore, which, just as a reminder, is what you're supposed to be helping me with, remember?"

"Oh yeah," Jaime says. "We missed the turn back there."

He makes an about-face and walks back in the direction we just came from. We pass an artist drawing a caricature of a little girl with braided hair that I can see doesn't look anything like her. The girl looks really tired of smiling.

"Okay," I say to Jaime, "your turn. What are you doing here?"

"Tell you later."

Jaime takes a running leap and does a cartwheel with no hands.

"Come on, Jaime, that's not cool. I totally spilled my guts—"

"Hey!" He interrupts me in the middle of my sentence. "What time is it?"

I sigh, but I look at my watch. "One oh three."

"Shoot!" he exclaims. "Shootshootshoot!"

CHAPTER 20

Jaime takes off running, then turns left down a smaller path. If I can barely keep up with him when he's walking, then I don't stand a chance when he's sprinting.

By the time I catch up to him—which I do only because he finally stops—my lungs are about to burst.

We're standing in an empty area, in between the Majestic Theater and a gift shop that sells customized magic wands. It's pretty deserted. He sits on a bench and pulls something out of his pocket.

I brace myself for a curling iron or a meat cleaver, but what he's pulling out is a walkie-talkie. A small, black, official-looking radio exactly like the one Schmidt was using. He turns a knob and it makes a crackly noise.

"What are you doing?" I whisper, sitting down next to him on the bench.

"You don't have to whisper," he says. "They can't hear us unless I press the TALK button."

"Where'd you get that?"

"Tell you later."

"I'm keeping track of the info you owe me, by the way," I say. "So don't think—"

"Shhhh. I can't hear."

"But nobody's talking."

"Exactly."

I have no idea what he's talking about, which is a familiar feeling by now. So I just get up and walk over to the water fountain nearby because it's about 150 degrees and I feel like I've just run a marathon. Jaime, on the other hand, hasn't even broken a sweat.

When I get back to the bench, I ask, "Where are we, anyway?"

He stands and points over the top of a high row of bushes to our left. I make out the back side of the security booth with the Valuables Lost and Found. Then Jaime starts talking, fast.

"Okay, I know you love plans, so I got one for you. You ready?"

I nod.

"Step 1: You run into the Lost and Found and get your backpack."

I wait for him to continue, but that's it. That's the whole plan.

"That's not a plan. That's a telegram."

"What's a telegram?"

"You don't—"

He shakes his head. "Whatever, not the point. You ready?"

"No!" I almost shout. "What about Schmidt? How am I supposed to get by him?"

"Schmidt's going to run out of that security booth in a minute, and he's going to leave in a hurry, which means he probably won't lock the door on his way out."

"Annnnnd?"

"And you're going to run in, grab the backpack, and run back here."

"What if someone else is there?"

"No one will be there."

"What about dogs? Police dogs?"

Jaime tilts his chin down and stares at me for a long second without saying anything. "What if your backpack is being guarded by police dogs? For real?"

I shrug. "It's possible."

"Well, *yeah*," Jaime says. "Anything's *possible*. But I think police dogs probably have better stuff to do. Like catching drug lords and all that."

He shakes his head. "Why am I even talking about this? There are no police dogs here. You're getting us off track."

"*I'm* getting us off track?" I say. In all the time I've spent with Jaime, I don't think he's even been within miles of the track.

"Listen, we don't have much time. The Captain takes his lunch break exactly at one o'clock. He only takes about fifteen minutes. He eats in about five and spends the rest of the time doing high-impact calisthenics while listening to Metallica."

At first I think he's joking because it's too weird to be true and also, how could Jaime possibly know this? But he's looking dead serious.

"How do you—" I start.

"Tell you later." He's pulling me to my feet, and pushing me over to the bushes. "The point is, when he's listening to Metallica, he's not listening to the walkie-talkie. And I need him not listening when I do this—"

He presses the TALK button on the side and starts speaking. Except it doesn't sound like him. His voice comes out all deep and gravelly, and it's got a strong twang.

"Captain to base," he growls. "Do you copy?"

I don't know what I was expecting him to do, but it was not this. I'm staring at him and I'm making gestures that are supposed to communicate, "Stop! Halt! Go no further!"

But Jaime's not looking at me. And now Schmidt's voice is coming through.

"Schmidt to Captain. I copy. Are you enjoying your lunch, sir?"

"Schmidt!" Jaime's voice booms out.

"Y-yes, yessir?"

"We got ourselves a situation at Tsunami Falls. I have eyes on Boy Wonder. Requestin' backup pronto. Bring the whole crew."

I've only heard the Captain's voice a few times, so I can't say for sure how close this imitation is, but it seems spot-on. Schmidt is definitely buying it.

"Yessir. Copy that. Let me just—"

"NOW!" Jaime yells. He lets go of the TALK button and tells me, "Soon as he comes out, go straight through the bushes."

I peek through a small gap in the bushes and fix my eyes on the back door of the booth. A few seconds later, the door flies open, so hard that it swings back fast and hits Schmidt full-on in the face. He yowls like a dog, grabs his forehead, and hobbles toward the security cart parked a few steps away.

"Guys!" he hollers. "Captain wants everyone. Get in!"

A handful of security guards standing in a cluster nearby rush over to the cart. Schmidt is so nervous he drops the keys, twice, before he manages to put them in the ignition. But finally the packed security cart rushes toward Waterworld.

"Are you waiting for an engraved invitation?" Jaime whispers, pushing me through the gap in the bushes. "Go! Go! Go!"

My heart is slamming against my chest like a jackhammer, but I don't have time to worry about whether I'm having a heart attack, because I'm too busy running full-speed toward the back door of the booth. I'm keeping an eye out for police dogs, but it looks like Jaime was right—there's not a canine in sight.

There are also no security guards. The coast is clear.

I consider slowing down and just casually walking into the booth, which might be a little less suspicious, but I'm too nervous. I just want this to be over. So I run at breakneck speed through the back door and pull it shut behind me.

It's really cold in the booth, like the air conditioner's working overtime. There is a metal shelving unit full of stuff—backpacks, purses, fanny packs—and bins filled with wallets and jewelry and lots of cell phones. There is way more stuff than I expected.

I look through the shelves as quickly as I can, but they're not organized, which bothers me. They should be organized. It would be so easy to do—wallets and cell phones on top, fanny packs on the next shelf, backpacks below that. I have to fight the urge to stop in the middle of the heist and hunker down to sort everything.

Pull it together, I tell myself. *Think like a criminal.*

I double-check the shelves, but my yellow backpack is nowhere to be found. I'm totally stumped, and also I can't tell how much time has passed. I didn't have a chance to check my watch before. Maybe it's only been thirty seconds, but maybe it's been five minutes—I have no idea. I wish I could ask Jaime what to do because Jaime always seems to know what the next move is. I'm just about to give up and leave when I remember that the last time I saw my backpack, Schmidt was holding it, in the front part of the booth. Maybe it's still there.

There's a door straight ahead of me and another door a few feet away, off to the side a little. The booth is bigger than it looks from the outside, with a bunch of different rooms inside. I look from one door to the other, feeling like I'm defusing a bomb, choosing which wire to cut. I decide to see what's behind door number one and rush through to what turns out to be—joy of joys—the front part of the booth. I notice three things right away:

1. My backpack is on the floor under the counter. I could reach out and grab it.
2. There's a customer waiting on the other side of the glass.
3. The customer is Priya's little sister.

I haven't seen Zara in over a year, but it is definitely her. She is one of the most recognizable people I've ever met—pretty much the opposite of me. Mainly this is because she has eyes that are two different colors—one brown and one blue. She looks a lot older than the last time I saw her, and I figure she's got to be almost nine by now.

I stand there, all deer-in-the-headlights, without

saying anything. I am sure she'll recognize me, and I am also sure that if she's here, Priya is here, too, and Priya's parents.

Zara is talking, but my mind is so busy making sense of all this, I don't hear her.

"What?" I croak.

"Do you work here?"

Incredibly, she doesn't seem to know who I am. I realize I'm still wearing the bucket hat and pink sunglasses, plus my hair is totally different. Maybe that's all it takes to go incognito—at least, enough to fool a nine-year-old.

"Umm, no, sorry." I lean over, grab my backpack, and sling it over my shoulder.

"Then what are you doing in there?" She crosses her arms in front of her chest. Zara hasn't changed one bit. She's as assertive as ever.

"Oh, right, yeah. No, I mean, I *do* work here, but I'm, uhh, on break. Someone else is coming in a minute." I try to disguise my voice by making it higher and more nasal. It's not terribly convincing. I definitely do not have Jaime's voice-distortion skills.

"But I need help now. I lost my sister's inhaler, and if we don't find it *right now* my mom says we have to go home because my sister can't be here without her inhaler."

"Right," I say. "Hey, where are your parents?" I don't want to waste precious time continuing this conversation, but I also need to know if I'm about to run smack into the whole Kumari family.

"They're right over there." She gestures to the Majestic Theater. "Looking for the inhaler. They think maybe we left it there."

"We haven't found any inhalers," I tell her, walking to the door.

"But it's in my sister's backpack. A zebra-striped backpack."

Zebra stripes? I can't help but think. *Since when does Priya wear zebra-print accessories?*

"I was wearing it, and I put it down somewhere, but I forgot where, and now we lost the backpack with the inhaler, and they're all mad at me."

"Yeah, we don't have any zebra backpacks," I tell Zara. "I was just looking, and there's nothing like that."

It happens to be the truth, but even if it wasn't, I'd tell Zara the inhaler was gone because I need her family to hightail it out of Foreverland as fast as humanly possible.

"Oh noooo," Zara moans. Then she starts to cry.

Fun fact: Only a truly heartless person can abandon a crying kid.

Related fact: I am not a truly heartless person.

I have to get out of this booth immediately. There is a long list of people who are going to show up here any second who I desperately need to avoid—Priya, her parents, a fleet of angry security guards who've just been pranked.

But I can't just leave Zara crying like this.

"Hey, it's okay," I say. "Don't cry, Zara."

As soon as the words are out of my mouth, I realize my mistake.

So does Zara. She looks up, startled, and starts to ask, "How do you—"

But it's too late. I'm dashing out of the booth and booking it into the bushes before she can even get the question out.

CHAPTER 21

As I fight my way through the tight gap in the bushes, my backpack gets stuck. I feel caught, like a fly in a spiderweb. A part of me is relieved, because, let's face it, being a fugitive is totally exhausting. I sort of want the whole heist to be over.

But Jaime's there on the other side of the bushes, and he yanks on my arm until the backpack comes loose.

I tumble to the ground with a racing heart and a stitch in my side. The concrete scrapes my knee, which stings a lot and starts to ooze a little blood. I try to catch my breath while Jaime grabs the back-pack off my shoulder and stuffs the whole thing into a big plastic Foreverland shopping bag he magically produces out of thin air.

"Took you long enough," he grumbles.

I want to reply, but I'm still panting and my knee hurts. Talking is too much effort.

Then he says "Shhhh!" even though I'm not talking. He holds the walkie-talkie up to his ear. The Captain—the real one, this time—is on a rant.

"JUST LIKE ME? The voice sounded JUST

LIKE ME? Do I have a TWIN running around, Schmidt? Do I have a DOPPLEGÄNGER?"

Then comes Schmidt's voice: "Captain, I'm so sorry. Almost back at base now."

"Time's up," says Jaime. "*Vámonos!*"

Jaime runs off, toward the center of the park, while I scramble to catch up, limping a little. He darts into a big crowd of little kids wearing orange Camp Dandelion T-shirts and caps, and for a minute I lose him. Then the group thins out, and I see the glint of his mirrored sunglasses as he looks back to find me. I run over to his side.

"Were you serving a *customer* back there?" Jaime shakes his head and makes a tsk-tsk sound. "Oh, Margarita."

"It wasn't a customer," I say, still panting. "It was a girl I know."

He stops walking so suddenly that a little boy walking behind him crashes right into Jaime's back.

"Did she recognize you?" he asks.

"No, but—" I start, but Jaime cuts me off with a loud whoop.

"I *told* you the makeover would work!" he says, walking again. "You should always listen to me. I am wise."

"Okay, Oh-Wise-One, but can I finish?"

I explain the situation with Priya's lost inhaler and how I called Zara by her name and everything. Jaime listens but doesn't seem troubled.

"I didn't see the backpack in the Lost and Found, so maybe they did really lose it, in which case they're going home, but maybe they've already found it, in which case they're staying. And that, in case you're wondering, would be bad, because Priya used to be my best friend, and she'll recognize—"

"What happened?"

"Huh?"

"You said she 'used to' be your best friend. So what happened?"

"Nothing," I say, more defensively than I mean to. "We went to different middle schools, and, you know, we just drifted apart or whatever."

"C'mon, Margarita," he says in this teasing way that should really annoy me but is actually kind of funny. "What'd she do? She steal your boyfriend or something?"

"What? No. What are you even—nothing, like, *happened*. She just—she's very friendly or whatever so she made a lot of new friends at her new school. And, you know, she's just busy with . . . that."

"So she ditched you." He shakes his head. "That's cold."

I roll my eyes at him. "You're a drama king, you know that? But you're focused on the wrong drama. You need to focus on how she's here, right now, and I might run into her at any minute. So I should probably take off."

"Hold up," he says, stopping again. "You're leaving?"

"Well, yeah, I guess so. I mean, I have my money now, so . . ."

"But I thought you hated being at home. I thought you couldn't stand it there."

"Sure, but—"

"So don't go back," he says, and then he adds, "I mean, not right this minute."

"But Priya's here—"

"So what? Her sister had a whole conversation with you and didn't recognize you."

"Yeah but—"

"We haven't even had any fun yet."

"I've had fun."

He takes off his sunglasses and fixes me with a hard stare. "You rode the carousel about a hundred times, and then you choked on a hot dog, and you spent the night holed up in an empty Haunted House."

"That's fun!" I protest, looking down at my feet. "That's definitely in the neighborhood of fun."

"That is not even close to fun. You'd need to take an airplane to get from *that* to fun."

He crosses his arms over his chest, like he's getting serious.

"Look, you can't leave right now anyway. The Captain has definitely realized the backpack is gone, and he'll be watching the exit like a hawk for a while.

In a few hours, when it all dies down, you can leave. I'll even help you get out without anyone noticing."

I don't say anything. I'm thinking. Or I'm trying to think. Jaime makes it hard to think. He's so sure about everything, it's impossible to imagine he might be wrong. But at the same time, I know he's bored and lonely and wanting company, so I don't know if I can trust his plan.

"I'm right." He gives me a wink and a smile. "You know I'm right."

It is a smile you can't argue with. Besides, he is right about one thing. I'm in an amusement park. I deserve a little amusement.

"Two rides," I say.

"Five."

"Three. It's my final offer."

"Three rides and a slushie," he says. "It's *my* final offer."

"You drive a hard bargain."

"It's what I'm known for. That and my makeovers."

CHAPTER 22

Jaime leads us through Sky City, over to the Magical Morsels food court, where he finally stops.

"Slushies first, or we could die of thirst," he says. "Save our table while I get them, okay? You look like a . . . watermelon—no, wait . . . I'm getting . . . a cherry vibe. Am I right?"

"Actually, I'm a blue raspberry kind of gal."

Jaime hits himself in the forehead.

"Right, right. The black sheep of the raspberry family. Okay, be right back."

He throws the Foreverland bag holding my backpack onto a table and heads over to the Cloud Café. I slide into the blue plastic booth and do an inventory check. Everything's still in my backpack: my money, train ticket, Darling, and my lucky rabbit foot.

Priya gave me this rabbit foot because of how superstitious I've always been. I've changed backpacks a few times, but I always keep the lucky rabbit foot. It's weird to think that the rabbit foot has lasted longer than our friendship.

I crack open my notebook and write:

Perfect. For a year, I've been dying to

Run into her

In the neighborhood,

Yet now that we're a whole state

Away, here she is.

I start to write an acrostic for Zara, but the sound of arguing makes me look up. A few tables away, a couple is fighting while their kid, a little boy in thick glasses, sits across from them, looking miserable. I recognize that defeated expression on his face. I've been there.

I turn back to my notebook but right away, I hear yelling. It's not coming from the couple, who are still bickering in low voices, but from the Cloud Café counter. It's the girl from yesterday—the short girl with the platinum pixie cut who was yelling at the Slushie Guy. But this time, she's not yelling at the Slushie Guy. She's yelling at Jaime.

She's wearing another punk-ified Foreverland staff T-shirt today. The sleeves have been lopped off and the elastic neck, too, so it's been made into a tank top. One side of the shirt's been slit open from armpit to waist, and then connected again with about a hundred safety pins. A chain of safety pins dangles from each of her hoop earrings.

Fun fact: No one needs this many safety pins.

Related fact: Safety pins are not safe in all situations.

I can't hear what she's saying, but it's pretty clear she's not happy, not happy at all. She crosses her arms in front of her while Jaime replies, gesturing a lot, which makes him look nervous. Then, suddenly, she spins around and stomps over to the slushie machine while Jaime waits. Her back is to me, so I can't see what she's doing, but when she turns around she's holding two big foam cups, which she carries over to the register and slams down on the counter in front of Jaime. She slams them so hard, the plastic tops pop off and the slushies slosh everywhere.

Jaime fixes the cups and then walks away fast, with Safety Pin Girl glaring after him. She has big, dark eyes that are flashing so much, it looks like she could electrocute someone with a sideways glance.

I watch her watching Jaime until he gets to my table. Then I watch her watch me. Which is pretty much the creepiest experience ever. She is like a human atom bomb.

Jaime slides into the booth across from me and hands me a cup.

"Check out this family over here," he says, nodding in the direction of Glum Glasses Boy. "Sometimes I wonder why people even get married."

It's a fair point and, honestly, I wonder the same

thing, but right now there's something a tad more urgent to discuss.

"Um, Jaime?" I say. "Who's the girl?"

He picks up a park map that someone left on our table, tears it down the middle so it rips into two even pieces. Then, on one piece, he scribbles something with a red marker he pulls out of his magical pocket.

"What girl?" he asks.

"*What girl?* Safety Pin Girl. Human Atomic Bomb Girl. Girl-Who-Makes-Me-Actually-Fear-for-My-Life Girl."

Jaime looks up from the map piece. "Wait, are you making eye contact with her? You, uhh, you really shouldn't do that."

"Jaime!" I whisper. "Explanation! Now!"

Jaime's folding the little map piece into some mysterious shape with fast, sure motions. "That's just Belle."

"Belle? She doesn't look like a Belle. She looks more like a Mephistopheles."

"She's all bark and no bite," he says, taking a slurp of his slushie. "Just, seriously, don't make eye contact with her . . . or tell her your real name . . . or, you know, where you live or anything like that."

He does not look like he's joking. The dial on my anxiety meter, which has been simmering at LO, gets jacked all the way up to HI. I get that old familiar thundery-heart, sweaty-palms feeling again.

Of course, Jaime could not look less worried. He picks up his folded creation, which turns out to be a paper airplane. He inspects it, then makes some adjustments.

"Ummm," I say. "Is there a reason we're still sitting here? Shouldn't we, you know, go? Like, to literally any other place but here?"

Jaime nods, like he's totally with me.

"I would, except that she said to stay. And, you know, when Belle gets like this, it's usually a good idea to do what she says."

I dare to look over at her again, but she's not looking at us anymore. She has her back turned and seems to be actually working.

"Does she . . ." I pause, choosing my words carefully. "Does she, like, *like* you?"

He looks genuinely horrified.

"Nonononono. She's an old friend."

"It's just, she seems really mad, like, I don't know . . . jealous? Or something?"

Jaime shakes his head. "Belle's just protective of me. She's my burger connection, you know. Without her, I'd have starved by now."

"So she knows you're crashing here?"

He nods. "The only way to pull this off is to have a connection."

"I don't have a connection," I point out.

"Yeah, you do," he says. "You have me."

Then he picks up the airplane and flicks his

wrist so that the paper sails, straight as an arrow, to the table of Glum Glasses Boy, whose parents are—big surprise—still arguing. The kid's face shifts from:

1. Miserable to
2. Surprised to
3. Delighted.

He unfolds the airplane and seems to read the message written there, because he bursts out laughing.

"What did you write?"

"Just a dumb joke," he says. "How do you make time fly?"

"How?"

"Throw a clock out the window."

The boy's smiling now and eating his lunch. His parents have even stopped arguing to check out the airplane. Boy Wonder saves the day.

"Hey, don't look now, but she's coming," Jaime warns. He turns to a leftover square of the map and sets to work on that piece—folding, unfolding, refolding. "Just let me do the talking."

I stare at Jaime's hands as they quickly twist and bend and flatten the paper. I stare hard while I listen to the sounds of what could be called footsteps, except that footsteps sound light! And lovely! Nothing like the sound of Belle walking toward us.

She is so small; I don't understand how her steps can be so heavy. They sound like certain doom.

Then the doom-steps stop. My eyes shoot down to the ground next to the table, and I see Belle's feet, which are, impossibly, in black combat boots. It's scorching hot today, and she's wearing leather boots. She's hung a bunch of safety pins off the boots' laces—just in case, you know, she runs out.

Suddenly there's a huge clattering, which is the sound of a tray full of food being thrown down on the table in front of me.

French fries fly in all directions. A burger-shaped bundle rolls onto my lap.

"Hungry?" Belle snarls. Then I look up—I can't help myself—and I instantly regret it. She is way, way more terrifying up close. Maybe it's the thick black eyeliner she's drawn on her lids or the fact that she smells like ash, like she just burned down a small village. Or maybe it's the belt she's wearing on her denim cutoff shorts, which has about a thousand spikes sticking out. The spikes do not look ornamental.

She is looking at me, like she's waiting for me to say something. So I do. For some unimaginable reason, I say, "Hi! I'm Margaret O'Shea! You must be Belle?"

I see Jaime wince a little.

Belle is giving me a look that is flat-out blood-thirsty, like she'd love nothing more than to chug down a large quantity of my blood. But before she can say anything, Jaime chimes in.

"Belle!" he sings, like he's genuinely happy to see her. "I made you something."

He tosses the origami creation up at her, and she catches it without missing a beat.

"A bird?" she asks.

"Like your tattoo," Jaime says. He nods at her calf, and, sure enough, there's a tattoo of a green-and-yellow bird. I'm not surprised that she has a tattoo, but I am surprised by the animal she chose. I wouldn't have pegged Belle as a bird-watcher. I would've thought she'd be into snakes or spiders or scorpions. Something with venom.

"Thanks," Belle says to Jaime. Or, at least, her mouth says that. Her eyes say, *"I will name this paper bird 'Margaret O'Shea' and light it on fire."*

As if to prove that, she leans over the table toward me. The ash smell gets stronger. Maybe she's fire-breathing, like a dragon.

"Like your slushie?" she purrs.

"Uh-huh," I say quickly. Then, like I have to prove it, I take a massive slurp. "*Re*freshing!"

"Good," she says. "I made it special for you."

And that is when I realize that Belle has probably poisoned me.

First, a hot dog nearly kills me. Now, a slushie.

My mom was right. I really should stay away from fast food.

I try to remain calm as she straightens up again and turns to walk back to the counter. But, like in a horror movie when you think the bad guy is dead but it turns out he's still got life in him, she turns around again and smiles at me. It is a smile that Lucifer himself would have been jealous of. That's how evil it is.

"Have a magical day," she says.

CHAPTER 23

As soon as she turns her back again, I start coughing and clearing my throat because suddenly, the slushie has a very weird aftertaste, and I'm not sure, but I suspect that taste may be arsenic. Meanwhile Jaime's mouth is just fine, never better. He's devouring the fries and one of the burgers she brought us.

"Do you think—I mean—" I stammer. "Is it possible that your friend, like, actually poisoned me?"

Jaime laughs so hard he starts choking on his burger. I think for a second that I'm going to have to whack his back this time. But he takes a big gulp of his slushie, and that seems to do the trick.

"You're funny."

And I go with that interpretation.

"See, Belle's like a tarantula," he says, biting into a fry.

"I agree," I say. "She's deadly and should be avoided at all costs."

He shakes his head as he chews a huge bite of burger. "Tarantulas get a bad rap. They're actually really friendly. Make great pets. Looks can be deceiving."

Jaime polishes off the rest of his burger.

"So Belle just looks scary?" I say. "But really, she's sugar and spice and everything nice?"

"Sure, if you consider black pepper a spice." He licks some ketchup off his top lip. "But for real, Belle's cool. Trust me."

"Okay, fine. Whatever. Hey, are we free to leave now?" I ask. "Or are we still being detained?"

"We're good." He points to my burger, which I haven't touched. "Are you going to eat that?"

I shake my head. I was only half joking about Belle poisoning me, and I don't feel like taking any chances. So Jaime slips the burger into his bottomless pocket. I wouldn't be surprised to discover he has a fridge in there, or a microwave.

"Okay," he says, standing. "Let's roll."

He walks out of the Magical Morsels area, and I, of course, follow. The park is really crowded, but Jaime takes us down a little shady path that's not so packed. Now that we're out of Belle's nuclear blast zone, I feel more relaxed.

"Hey, what time is it?" he asks.

I look at my watch. "Two thirteen."

He breathes out loudly. "It's the worst time for lines. So maybe we start with Vertigo Vortex. That line will be long but it'll move fast. Or we could do Parachute Plunge. That line's never too bad. Then later, we'll do the Shooting Star. After four, the lines are better."

We walk over a little bridge into Waterworld. I can hear the crash of the waterfall nearby, from Tsunami Falls.

"Yeah, the thing is," I tell Jaime. "I don't . . . I'm not a big fan of roller coasters."

"What does that mean?"

"I, uhh, don't ride them."

He stops in his tracks and pulls down his sunglasses, then tips his chin so he's looking at me over the tops of the mirrored lenses.

"You're joking, right?"

I shake my head.

"You ran away to an amusement park but you don't ride roller coasters?" He says it slowly, like it's a riddle he's trying to solve.

"It's not a big deal. I like a lot of the other rides. All the spinning ones. The carousel. The Ferris wheel."

But he's not listening to me. He's grabbing my elbow and leading me to the nearest bench.

"This is worse than I thought," he says. "You need an intervention."

"I don't need an intervention," I tell Jaime. "I just don't want to strap myself in a hunk of metal that goes from zero to eighty miles in under ten seconds. Malfunctions happen. They happen all the time. Did you know that every year, more than four thousand kids are injured on amusement park attractions? Just in America?"

Jaime looks like he's considering this.

"How many people are injured in car crashes every year?"

"I don't know exactly—"

"You think it's more than four thousand?"

I sigh. "Probably."

"But you still ride in cars."

He makes this "*I rest my case*" gesture, like he's totally nailed this argument.

I sigh again, louder this time. "Look, this was a nice pep talk or whatever. But you're not the first to try this genius strategy on me. My parents have tried. Teachers. Professionals, even." I wipe sweat from my forehead. "When I was little, I was terrified of tornadoes—which is what happens when you watch *The Wizard of* Oz too early, by the way—"

"That's a freaky movie. Those flying monkeys?" He shudders.

"Yeah, I know. But for me, the tornado was the scary part. My mom was all about using logic and reason to, like, talk me out of the fear. And my dad flat-out promised it wouldn't happen. He kept saying, 'We live in New York City. Never gonna happen.' And then, like a month later, guess what happened a block from my apartment?"

"No way," Jaime says. "A tornado?"

"Yep. And after, when I asked my dad why he lied to me, he was like, 'I didn't lie. I made a mistake. Sometimes parents make mistakes.' Which was, looking back, the understatement of the century.

And after that, I was so terrified, I didn't even want to leave the house for a while."

Jaime thinks about this for a second. Then he says, "You worry too much."

"You're just figuring this out now?"

He rattles off a list, counting each item on his fingers, like he's keeping a tally: "Tornadoes, rocking Ferris wheel cars, lice, rabies—"

"Scabies."

"Whatever, scabies. And that's all fine—be totally terrified of that stuff, who cares? But you cannot be scared of roller coasters." He crosses his arms over his chest. "I won't let you."

I cross my arms right back. And then I laugh because it is, honestly, so ridiculous. "You won't let me? Who are you, the king of Foreverland?"

"Nope, that job's already taken. Nicky's been the king all summer."

"Oh, is that his name? Long hair, hunched shoulders? Looks so bored he can barely breathe?"

"Yeah, that's Nicky."

"Okay, it's official," I say. "You are a Foreverland expert."

"Yeah, I am. And as an expert, I have to say, for real—"

He sits down next to me on the bench and looks at me so intently, it's like he's about to reveal the secret of the universe.

"You can't be afraid of roller coasters, Margaret.

They're . . ." He shakes his head fast. "I can't explain it. It's like, for those few seconds that you're riding, nothing else exists. You have no brain. You have no memories. The only moment that matters is the moment you're in."

Jaime is an excellent salesman. He could sell a T-bone steak to a vegetarian. He's totally transported by this speech, and I am, too. I spend most of my time wishing I was in the past or worrying about the future. The idea of being sucked into the moment, completely pulled in—well, it sounds really good. I'd like to know what that feels like.

"Okay," I tell him.

"You'll try a roller coaster?"

I nod, and he immediately starts whooping loudly.

"Shhhh!" I warn him. "Low-profile, remember? Besides, you haven't heard my conditions."

"Shoot."

"First we do the rides I want. Then I'll try the Catapult."

The Catapult is the smallest roller coaster in the park. Gwen has been trying to persuade me to ride it for years, always pointing to all the little kids waiting in line. It doesn't do any loops or go upside down. It's my best bet for an easy ride.

"Okay," says Jaime.

"And," I add, "if we see Priya or any of the other Kumaris, I am *out*. Got it?"

"You are not going to regret it, Margarita," he is saying, pulling me to my feet.

I wince. "I hate it when people say that."

"Let me guess—bad luck?"

"It's the *definition* of bad luck."

CHAPTER 24

Fun fact: Jaime has guts of steel.

We ride the spinning teacups four times, and we turn that wheel at velocities even NASA hasn't heard of, but still, when we get off, he doesn't so much as stumble.

Next, we hit the flying elephants and a bunch of other kiddie rides. It surprises me that Jaime's up for riding these, because most serious roller coaster people don't want to waste time on kiddie rides. But Jaime seems to genuinely love all the rides—even Baby Hells Angels, which we're not allowed to go on, because we're too old.

"But I'm six years old," Jaime tells the ride operator. He lisps so that "six" sounds like "thix."

The ride operator, a super-skinny old man with totally white hair and a white beard, says, "You're a five-foot-tall six-year-old?"

"Yeth," Jaime lisps. "I'm juth tho tall!"

The ride operator just shakes his head and waves us away, like he's been dealing with pests like us for a hundred years.

"That ith tho unfair!" Jaime pretends to pout as

we walk away. It's silly but it cracks me up. Jaime *does* act like a six-year-old sometimes.

"How old *are* you?" I ask him. He seems to be just about my age, but I can't really tell.

Jaime answers, but I don't hear him because Baby Hells Angels has started and a real six-year-old is laying on his horn for a full minute. When the kid finally stops honking, Jaime's on to the next thing.

"Let's go to the Tree House," he says. "I gotta get something."

"You've gotta *get* something? In the Tree House?"

But Jaime's already halfway to the Tree House entrance, and by the time I catch up with him, he's on all fours, crawling into the tunnel at the front.

The Tot Town Tree House is plastic, not wood, and it's not built into an actual tree or anything—but it's still really cool because it's enormous. I follow Jaime through the tunnels on the ground, and then up a ladder, through some more tunnels, up another ladder—this one made of rope—which takes us to the very top.

At the top of the ladder is a tiny room, about as big as a Ferris wheel car. I can't stand up in it, so I crawl around on my knees. It reminds me of Rapunzel's tower because it's so high up, and there's a little window, too.

"This is awesome," I say.

"You've never been up here, right?"

"No. When I was little, I was too scared to climb this high, and then when I was old enough . . ."

"It seemed too babyish?"

I shrug. "Yeah, I guess."

"I know," Jaime says. "That's how everyone feels. Which is why this place is pretty much always empty even though it's super cool."

"You can see everything from up here." I'm looking out the window at the rest of the park, and I find Schmidt's security booth. There's a security cart parked out front, but just one. "Looks like things have died down at security. It's probably almost time for me to take off."

I really don't want to go, but I'm running out of ways to avoid feeling guilty about making my parents worry back at home.

"After the Catapult, though," Jaime reminds me.

I turn from the window to tell him yeah, sure, I'm not going to wimp out, but I stop short when I see that Jaime's digging around inside the floor. One of the floorboards has been lifted off, and his hand is reaching into the hole.

"A secret hiding spot? Really?"

"Well, I asked for a locker, but they don't give those to runaways," he shoots back.

I peer into his hiding spot then. It's a little space, not much bigger than a shoebox, but it's deep and there's all sorts of stuff piled up. Clothes, another walkie-talkie, a crumpled-up backpack. This is what

Jaime's looking for, I guess, because he pulls it out and empties it onto the floor. There's not much in it—a flashlight, a few bags of potato chips, some origami, and a travel-sized sewing kit.

"You sew?" I ask. "Is that part of your makeover package?"

"Very funny," he says, shaking out the rest of the stuff from the backpack. "I've got a hole in my sock, but I can't get the thread to go into the stupid needle."

"Give it to me."

"Really?" He looks skeptical but he takes off his shoe, pulls off his black sock, then tosses it to me.

"Ewww, it's *damp*," I say.

"This is when I remind you that I saved your life yesterday."

"Fair enough," I say. In a minute, I have the needle threaded and knotted and I'm sewing up the hole in the toe.

Jaime watches me. "Where'd you—"

"You're not the only one with tricks up your sleeve."

There's the sound of footsteps getting louder and then a grunting sound from the base of the ladder. Jaime speeds over and sits at the top of the ladder, blocking the entrance to the little room. He peers down at whoever it is below.

"Hey, move over," comes a kid's voice.

"Sorry," I hear Jaime say. "This room is closed for maintenance."

"Says who?"

I watch Jaime pull the walkie-talkie out of his pocket.

"Do I need to call security on you?" he growls.

There is a sigh and then the voice yells, "Fine!" I hear a thud, which I guess is the kid jumping down off the ladder and heading somewhere else.

"Intimidating little kids," I say. "Nice."

"All in a day's work," says Jaime. Then he tosses me the empty camo backpack. "You can move your stuff over into that, so you don't have to carry a shopping bag all over the park."

I toss the fixed-up sock at Jaime. Then I shake out all the stuff from my backpack onto the floor and start putting stuff in the camo backpack.

Jaime picks up my Creamsicle hand sanitizer and sniffs it.

"Think you got enough antibacterial stuff here?" he teases. "Maybe we should get more."

"Ha, ha, ha," I say flatly. "We'll see who's laughing when you get typhoid fever."

"You're gonna laugh when I get typhoid fever?" he asks. "That's cold."

I roll my eyes as I fold my change of clothes and place them in the backpack. "You know what I mean."

Jaime picks up Darling and looks at her thoughtfully.

"That's Darling," I say, and then I sigh. "Go ahead.

Tease me for bringing my lovey. I don't care. I never leave a bunny behind."

Jaime surprises me by rubbing one of Darling's ears between his fingers, then patting the top of her head gently.

"I'm not gonna tease you," he says. "I was just thinking about my own Darling. He was a rooster, not a bunny. And his name wasn't Darling. It was Peter."

"Peter the rooster."

"Yeah," he says quietly. "I wish I still had him."

"Lemme guess," I say. "Your mom accused you of hoarding stuff, then launched into a massive spring-cleaning and made you give him to Goodwill? Tale as old as time."

"Actually, I got rid of him myself. I was angry . . . and let's just say he didn't go peacefully. Scissors were involved."

I wince. "Poor Peter."

"Poor Peter," he repeats. Then he shakes his head, like he wants to shake the memory out, and focuses instead on putting on his new-and-improved sock.

I'm nearly done moving my stuff into the camo backpack. I unzip the front compartment to put my wallet in, and I see there's something in there. A photo.

My heart starts to pound because I know, right away, that Jaime won't want me to see it. But he's busy putting on his sneaker, and it's too late, I'm already looking at it. The picture was taken in Foreverland, in front of the Shooting Star. In the center is Jaime, but he's younger and wearing a yellow hard hat. Standing next to him is a man who's also wearing a hard hat. I'm sure it's his dad because he looks just like Jaime—same black wavy hair, same dark eyes, and the same ear-to-ear smile. The smiles aren't the kind of plastic, fake ones you slap on for posed pictures. The smiles, both of them, look real.

"You did a *darn* good job," Jaime is saying. "Get it? Dar—"

His voice breaks off and he lunges across the tiny room, grabbing the picture out of my hand.

"Sorry, it was just, I found it in the backpack," I say. "Is that your dad?"

Jaime slides the picture into his pocket and starts quickly throwing all the stuff on the floor into the hole, including the shopping bag and my old yellow backpack.

"We gotta go," he says.

He puts the floorboard back down, jiggling it a little so it fits in place. Then he leaps down the ladder hole. If I tried that move, I'd be in a cast. I'm guessing he lands on his feet, because all I hear is a soft thud and his voice calling, "C'mon, c'mon, c'mon!"

CHAPTER 25

Even though I only agreed to three rides, I spend the whole afternoon riding one after another with Jaime. He doesn't mention this and neither do I. I'm having fun, and I haven't had fun in, well, a long time. So I figure I'm overdue. I'll go home soon. And really, what difference does an hour or two make?

Everywhere we go, I look for Priya and her family, but there's no trace of them. We do see the Arts and Science girls' basketball team once, and twice I see security carts patrolling the area, but they don't get near us. My bucket hat blows off on Sky Seats, and I leave the pink sunglasses in one of the ride cubbies, but I don't need the full incognito outfit anymore. It seems like the fugitive hunt has died down.

Jaime keeps trying to get me on the Catapult, and I tell him, yes, for sure, but first I want to do a few more non-roller-coaster rides. When we ride all of those, I'm still not ready for the Catapult, so we go to Games. Since Jaime doesn't have any friends in high places here, we use my money.

I'm inserting ten dollars in the machine, which is blinking *CHANGE CHANGE CHANGE*, and Jaime says, "This machine freaks me out. I always feel like it's ordering me to change my evil ways or something."

Fun fact: Finding out that the kooky thoughts bouncing around inside your head are also bouncing around in someone else's head is a huge relief.

I must be really staring at Jaime, because he says, "I know, it's weird. Hey, your change is ready."

We blow through the change in way less time than we think we will. Then we sit on a bench in a little grassy area, and since we're hungry, we split the burger Belle gave us earlier, which is soggy but good. I make Jaime eat his half first, just in case I was right about her homicidal tendencies. While I eat, he makes the wrapper into a little origami frog.

"You're pretty good at that," I say.

He shrugs. "It's just something my dad taught me to do, so I could keep my hands busy. I don't like sitting still."

I am about to ask him when the last time he talked to his dad was, because it seems like his dad's the kind that would be worried about him. Before I can say anything, though, Mr. Doesn't-Sit-Still is on his feet.

"CataPULT! CataPULT! Now! Now! Now!"

"Jaime," I break in. "Listen, I'll *try* to go on the Catapult."

"Nuh-uh-uh!" Jaime is wagging his finger at me. "You're *going*. You promised."

"Well, I didn't exactly—"

"You can totally do this," he says. "Do you believe it?"

I shrug. "Sure, yeah, fine."

He shakes his head. "You either believe it or you don't. So . . . do you believe it?"

"No!" I shoot back. "Of course I don't!"

He looks me directly in the eye for a few seconds. "That's your problem right there. You gotta stay positive."

"Ugh," I groan. "You sound like my mother."

As soon as I say the word *mother*, I feel a stab of guilt pierce me, because I'd told myself this morning that I'd be home by now. I've stayed way longer than I should have.

I can't help but hear the almost begging way my mom would yell my name when I'd hide in the closet. She was, she *is*, so tough, so controlled. I've never seen her shed a single tear, not even when my grandfather died. The only moments I've ever seen her seem small and weak were those times she couldn't find me. I know that's how she must be feeling now, only way, way worse. And no matter how much I try to convince myself that she deserves it, I know she doesn't.

Jaime is snapping his fingers in front of my face, as if to wake me from a spell.

"Hellooooo? Are you ignoring my straight talk right now?" He raises his eyebrows at me. "Because I've had a breakthrough about you."

"A breakthrough?" I repeat. I'm still thinking about my mom and trying to figure out how to tell Jaime I need to leave really soon. I'm also trying to figure out how to motivate myself to do that. Because right now, it's the last thing I want to do.

"A breakthrough!" Jaime announces, throwing his hands in the air like a ringmaster. "Watch—and learn!"

He turns from me and takes off running across a grassy patch of lawn next to us. Once he's at top speed, he launches himself into the air and does a no-hands somersault in midair, then lands solidly on his feet.

He saunters back over to me, enormously pleased with himself.

"Know how I did that?"

"Ummm, years of practice?"

"Wrong!" he says. "The power of positive thinking."

I bust out laughing so hard, I snort. He does not laugh with me. "Oh, I'm sorry," I say. "Are you being serious?"

"I believe I can do it," he explains. "And I can do it."

I clap my hands together and look up at the sky. "I understand now!" I say, making my voice super high and wispy. "You just think happy thoughts! And up you go!"

He shrugs. "It's an attitude problem, plain and simple."

I laugh. "I'm sorry. I just—I'm not a 'think happy thoughts' kind of person."

"That might be the saddest thing I've ever heard."

"Okay, okay! I'm thinking of raindrops on roses and whiskers on kittens! Yay! See how happy I am?" I twist my face into a super-happy party-time grin, then let it drop. "I'll try the Catapult. Just no more inspirational talks, I beg you."

I decide that after the Catapult, I'll tell Jaime it's time for me to catch my train. I'll head home, soaring on the glory of that roller coaster ride.

"Okay, let's go," Jaime says. As we turn in the direction of Sky City, Jaime is smiling and nodding his head. "Whiskers on kittens. You gotta admit that's cute."

CHAPTER 26

The line for the Catapult is really long and we have time to kill, so I teach Jaime how to write acrostics. He writes one of his name:

Joker

And

Imposter.

Mouth always running.

Everywhere and nowhere.

When I read it, I don't know what to say. It feels too personal, like I just read his diary or something. And it seems sad, too. Sadder than I expected.

"Okay, Margarita, now do one of your name."

He passes me the pen and notebook.

"That's, like, the one acrostic I can't do," I say. "But here, I'll do one for Belle."

I scribble:

Bombs

Exploding and

Lightning striking are way

Less scary than this girl.

Even her eyeliner's atomic.

This makes Jaime launch into a perfect impression of Belle.

"This poem," he says, making his voice higher and his eyes narrow, "is dead wrong." Then he purses his lips tight and cocks his head to the side. "My eyeliner's not *atomic*. It's nuclear. YOU'RE AN AMATEUR!"

"Shhh!" I tell him. But I am laughing so hard, I choke on my own spit.

"Here's what I don't get," I say when I catch my breath. "How has she not been fired yet? Even just for the uniform violations. I mean, all those safety pins?"

"She can't be fired," Jaime says with this "duh" tone of voice, like it's so obvious. "Her dad owns the park."

"Belle's dad *owns* the park?"

"Yeah, of course," Jaime says. He takes the blue yo-yo from yesterday out of his pocket, and within a few seconds, the yo-yo's become a blue blur moving through the air under his hand. "Her dad makes her work here every summer, so, you know, she knows the value of a dollar," he explains. "But nobody can fire her."

"See, *this* is why I hang out with you," I say. "You know all the gossip."

"Well, that and the makeovers."

"Obviously." We move forward in line and turn a corner. A jolt of worry runs through me because I think we must be coming to the front of the line, but it just turns out to be another long section. We're nowhere near the front. I decide to take my mind off the certain doom that awaits me, and gossip seems like a good distraction.

"So, Jaime, gimme more dirt. Do you have anything on Schmidt?"

"Well, Schmidt's a lifer." Jaime makes the yo-yo shoot out into a circle, almost hitting the little kid in back of him. "He puts the forever in Foreverland, he's been working here that long. The park is his life—well, the park, that video game he loves, and his mom. She bakes the best blondie brownies you have ever tasted."

"It's kind of weird that you know that."

"I already told you." Jaime grins. "I know everything."

He flicks his wrist up, tossing the yo-yo, string and all, into the air above his head. Then he spins around in place and, incredibly, catches the yo-yo on its way down.

"So what about the Captain? There's got to be more about him."

Jaime shrugs. "He's new. He just started a few months ago, and he's all about running a tight ship. Pretty much everyone hates him. I mean, there's not much to like."

"Yeah, I noticed that the kid running the carousel was not a big fan."

"Oh, Jed. Yeah, Jed hates the Captain because Jed's constantly sucking face with Lily, who runs the Haunted House—"

I let out a little squeal.

"Tiny Braid Girl!"

Jaime gives me a confused look.

"Blue-streaked hair, tiny braids, wears lime-green Converse?"

"It's kind of weird you know that," he says, mimicking me from a minute ago. Usually, I hate to be teased, but when Jaime does it, it feels like a compliment.

"I guess you're not the only expert around here," I tease him back.

"Oh, so you wanna do this?" he says, grinning. "Foreverland Trivia. Round one. The Shooting Star's top velocity is . . . ?"

"Uhhhhhh . . ."

Jaime makes a loud buzzer noise. "Wrong! The correct answer is eighty miles an hour. And—I bet you don't know this, either—it only takes ten seconds for it to reach maximum velocity. That's what makes it possible for the ride to do three consecutive loop de loops, which—in case you didn't know—is a big deal."

"You do know that there's no way I'm ever stepping foot on the Shooting Star, right?"

"Never say never."

"How about never ever, ever? Can I say that?"

"It's criminal to come here and not ride the Shooting Star."

"Then go ahead and cuff me. Because I am *never* riding it."

"Even if I told you they invented a brand-new metal alloy just for this ride?"

Then he's off again, talking about lift hills and launch systems and electromagnetic propulsion. Jaime must notice that I'm not talking much, because he says, "Okay, yeah, I know it's boring, I'll shut up now."

"No, it's okay," I say. "I mean, I get it. I'm the same way about music boxes."

"Music boxes? With ballerinas and stuff?"

I grimace. "Noooo. Not those, like, extra-pink jewelry-box ones that people always give to five-year-old girls. I like old-fashioned music boxes, the kind you crank by hand."

Then it's my turn to geek out about hurdy-gurdies and band organs and calliopes.

Jaime listens for a while—longer than I figure he will—and then he says, "You need to get out more."

"Trust me, if you saw one of the really gigantic ones up close, like a Wurlitzer, you'd think it was cool. Actually, they have one here, in the park."

Jaime shakes his head. "I doubt it."

"No, they do," I insist. "In the middle of the Grand Carousel. It's what makes the music."

"Ohhhhhhhh," says Jaime. "*That's* what you're talking about? My dad always called that the One-Man Band."

I'm so busy wondering about this clue he just dropped, and trying to figure out a not-awkward way to ask him about it, that I don't notice we've crept up to the front of the line.

Suddenly, there are just two people in front of us. I can see the track. Two-seater cars are rolling in, full of laughing, shrieking people who hop off onto the opposite platform. Then the empty cars roll a few feet forward to pick up new victims.

My mouth instantly gets super dry, and at the same time, my palms start to sweat. It's like the moisture is pulled straight out of my mouth and into my hands for some reason. I know this feeling. I know it's just the beginning, the first embers of a blazing fire. So I try to get a handle on my panic.

This is no big deal, I tell myself. *The Catapult is basically a roller coaster with training wheels.*

That's what Gwen always used to say. I think of Gwen and imagine what her face will look like when I tell her I rode the Catapult. She will flip out, in the best way, I know. She'll stop texting Hugh for five minutes. She'll drop everything and order me to tell her all about it. I really want to be able to tell her I did it.

The duo ahead of Jaime and me gets in a car, and I watch it rush out of the station with what seems like a much-too-loud rumble. It sounds too heavy for the track. What if it *is* too heavy and one of the slats breaks? That must happen all the time. How could it not? Maybe that's what causes the four thousand injuries every year. What *were* those injuries, anyway? Some of them must have been little things—sprained ankles, broken arms—but some of them were probably more serious. Maybe a punctured lung. Broken neck. Severed head.

Don't think about severed heads, I think. And then, of course, they are all I can think about.

An empty car pulls up in front of us. Jaime jumps in, but I am not moving. I am just thinking about severed heads now, like, full-time. My stomach is all clenched up, and I feel suddenly so hot—the way you feel before you throw up.

"Margaret, come *on*," Jaime calls to me from the car. When I don't move, he marches back over and grabs me by the hand, leading me into the car. "A promise is a promise."

He's right. I did promise. So I make my feet move, and I step onto the car. And as soon as I do, all the air rushes out of my lungs, and I feel sort of like I did when I was choking on the hot dog, like I can't breathe. Jaime is telling me to sit, but I can't make my body bend.

I am standing in the car and gasping and pulling at the collar of my borrowed soccer jersey.

"You need to sit down," the ride operator calls to me.

I cannot sit down. I cannot even tell her that I can't sit down. All I can do is shake my head and gasp.

"Are you okay?" Jaime asks. Now he's standing up, too.

I keep shaking my head. Now I feel tears hitting my lips, so I guess I must be crying, but there are no crying noises, only the sound of this strangled gasping. I wonder if this is what it's like to be buried alive, because it feels like I am at the bottom of a deep hole, with not enough air, and now I'm thinking about dirt being thrown in my face, which is making everything even worse. And that's when Jaime grabs my hand and pulls me off the ride.

CHAPTER 27

Jaime leads me down the exit ramp to the cubbies, where he retrieves the camo backpack as I shuffle along behind him. Then he brings me to a bench and asks, "Wanna sit?"

I do want to sit. Now that I'm not on the roller coaster, the air is starting to reenter my lungs. It takes a minute before I can breathe normally again, and the whole time, Jaime doesn't say anything. I wish he would talk, because his silence makes this awkward situation about a million times more awkward. He just stands in front of me, with his arms crossed, and I can't tell if he's mad or what.

"I'm sorry," I pant. "I really—"

"Don't worry about it."

"You're not mad?"

He looks confused. "Why would I be mad? It's not your fault. Roller coasters just aren't your thing. Like, *really* not your thing. I didn't get it before but now I do. So . . ."

He jumps to his feet and rubs his hands together fast. "New plan!"

I raise my eyebrows. "There was an *old* plan?"

184

He tsk-tsks me. "Margarita, when will you learn?" Then he leans over and pulls me to my feet. He slings his arm over my shoulder and guides me away from the Catapult. "I *always* have a plan. Even when it seems like I don't. That's just part of the bigger plan."

"Yeah, right."

"I got a surprise for you."

"Jaime, I—"

"Nonono, it's not a ride," he assures me. But I wasn't going to say I didn't want to go on a ride. I was going to say I really need to go home.

"You are gonna love this!" he sings. "It's *perfect*!"

"I believe you, it's just—"

"Please, just let me show you this one thing." His voice is pleading now, his eyes hopeful. "I feel really bad I tried to make you go on that ride. That wasn't cool of me. Let me make it up to you."

I take a deep breath in and blow it out. "Sure."

The sun is low in the sky, and I know it's late, really late. I purposely do not look at my watch, because I'm trying to avoid the ever-growing guilty feeling I have about still being here. I should've been home hours ago.

After the surprise, I tell myself firmly. *No more stalling.*

I follow Jaime into the center of the park. I'm still keeping my eyes peeled for Priya and her family, but even if she found her inhaler earlier in the day, by now she'd probably have gone home. I'm glad I didn't bump into her, but in this weird way, I'm also a little bummed.

"What happened to you on that ride?" Jaime asks.

"I just started thinking about decapitated heads and—"

Jaime groans. "I said happy thoughts! *Happy!* Whiskers on kittens! Not decapitated people!"

"I didn't *mean* to. I just . . . my mind doesn't always go where I want it to."

"Tell me about it." He snorts. "My mind is never where it's supposed to be. Comes with the territory when you have ADHD. It got me into a lot of trouble at school. But it hasn't been a problem lately."

"You mean, because it's summer?"

"Something like that."

He's trying to be vague and mysterious, to make me curious. It works.

"How long have you been here, anyway?" I ask him.

But when Jaime doesn't want to answer a question, he just doesn't.

"School isn't my thing. The same way that roller coasters aren't your thing. That's how it is with me and school. My owl always ends up in the dirt."

"Your owl?"

We're passing through Waterworld now, and

there are hardly any lines for any of the rides—even Tsunami Falls. The park's emptying out.

"When I was in first grade, the teacher made us all cardboard owls with our names on them," Jaime says. "There was a tree on the blackboard, and all the owls would start off in the treetop, you know, where they belong. But if you screwed up— if you forgot to raise your hand, or you wouldn't sit down when you were supposed to, or you punched some stupid kid, even if he deserved it— well, your owl would move down a little. And if your owl hit the ground, then the teacher would call your parents."

"A great way to make kids hate owls."

"I know, right?" Jaime laughs. "So, by Christmas, my teacher had stopped putting my owl back up at the treetop every morning. She just left it at the bottom. She was like, 'Why bother? I know you're gonna end up there anyway.'"

"Jaime!" I say. "That's so unfair. How could they let her do that?"

He shrugs. "It wasn't her fault. I mean, I kept screwing up. I didn't mean to. I just did. And not just that year, either."

He springs forward a few steps and does a perfect hands-free cartwheel. "School's just not for me," he says again.

"Well, *that* school wasn't for you, maybe," I say. "There are other schools."

"It's okay." he says. "I didn't even care that I was a screwup—"

"Jaime," I say. "Don't call yourself that. It's not true."

He smiles. "Now you sound like my dad." He looks down and kicks at a big pebble on the path. "That was the worst part, actually—letting him down. I didn't want him to be disappointed."

"Yeah," I say. "I know that look. I feel like it's just my mom's permanent face now. The *'Really? That's the best you can do?'* face."

"So don't go back."

Jaime steps in front of me, blocking my way.

"Jaime," I say. "If I stay here tonight, my parents are going to lose their—"

He is shaking his head fast. "I don't mean that you should go back tomorrow. I mean that you shouldn't go back at all."

I snort loudly. "Yeah, right."

Jaime's chin is tilted down, and he's looking at me so intently with his dark eyes, it's like he's trying to perform hypnosis on me.

"Are you actually being serious?" I ask. He doesn't say anything.

"Jaime," I say. "Come *on*."

"I thought you were running away," he says. "Not just taking a little vacation."

There's a bite to his words that takes me by surprise.

"Well, yeah, I *was* running away," I say. "But I never thought I'd stay away for good. I mean, that's . . . to begin with, I'm almost out of money."

"You don't need money," he says. "We have Belle."

I can't believe he's serious. It makes me wonder how long he's been in the park. This whole time, I've thought he left home a few days ago, but now I'm worried it's been a lot longer.

"Jaime," I say. "How long have you been here?"

"Don't change the subject!" His words snap like a rubber band. "You said your parents are stupid and you don't want to be there."

"They are," I say. "I don't."

"So . . ." He raises an eyebrow. "Stay."

I look down at my sandals because I don't want to see the disappointment on his face when I tell him.

"I can't," I say, my voice low. "They're my family."

As I say it, I know that it's true.

When I look up at Jaime, his eyes have turned cold. He looks angry.

"Come on, Jaime," I plead, because I really don't want to fight, not now. "My parents are probably losing it right now and I—I feel bad. I mean, don't you?"

He flinches, like I've slapped him, even though I have no idea what I could have said wrong.

"No," he says, spinning away from me and walking forward again. He jams his hands, hard, into his shorts pockets. I follow after him, feeling like I want to say something but afraid that anything I say will make things even worse.

We're leaving Sky City now, and in the distance ahead of us, on Magic Mile, I can hear the sounds of drums and a crowd cheering.

I decide to change the subject. "The parade's starting."

"I know that," he snarls. "I know you think I'm an idiot, but I do actually have a plan, you know."

"I don't think—"

Jaime's whole body is stiff. He reminds me of a cat with its fur sticking straight up. I don't know what I did to upset him, but I have to head home soon and this isn't the way I want to leave things.

"So . . . are we going to the parade? Is that the surprise?"

He snickers. "No."

Jaime's walking fast toward the carousel, and I have to jog a little to catch up. We're smack in the center of the park, but there's hardly anyone around. From the sound of the cheering coming from Magic Mile, everybody with a pulse is at the parade.

"Are we going on the carousel?"

"You're a real detective there, Sherlock," he says, but not in a funny way. "What's the problem? I thought you liked the carousel."

"There's no . . . I *do* like the carousel."

"All right," he grumbles. "Just follow me, then."

Fun Jaime is pretty much the best company

around, and Angry Jaime is pretty much the worst. What's tripping me up is how sudden this change was. It's a real Dr. Jekyll and Mr. Hyde situation.

I've obviously hurt his feelings, but only because he misunderstood something, and I really want to clear things up before we say goodbye.

"Hey, Jaime?" I'm careful because I feel like I could set him off at any minute. "It's not that I don't want to, like, stay forever. That would be awesome. It's just . . . this isn't real life, you know? And I need to go back to my real life—I mean, so do you. You *are* going back, right? Eventually? To your dad or whatever?"

He ignores me. He's walking so fast, I'm talking to his back.

"Because—look, I don't know what happened with you guys and it's none of my business or whatever, but seriously, he's got to be really worried about you—"

Jaime stops short suddenly, so fast that I almost crash into him. He spins around to face me, and the rage on his face is so intense, I almost don't recognize him. It startles me and makes me step back. His mouth is all twisted up, and his dark eyes are flashing.

"Shut up! Just shut up! You don't know what you're talking about!"

He spits the words out. Like there's venom in each one.

"Okay."

Immediately, he seems sorry. He looks down at his feet and then he says, "I mean, it's just complicated, okay? It's not what you think."

"Okay."

"I just . . . see? There goes my owl. Facedown in the dirt." He breathes out loudly. "I'm sorry. For real. Okay? Is it okay?" He tries to catch my eye but I look away. "Anyway, don't you want to see the surprise? Come on, let's go, let's go, *vámonos!*"

Then, just like that, he's back to being happy-go-lucky Jaime. Like nothing happened.

Whatever, I think. *I'm leaving as soon as the surprise is over.*

There's no line for the carousel. Not one single person's waiting to get on. The ride operator is the same pimply, red-haired kid from yesterday—Jed. He's not standing by the gate. He's over to the side, standing next to the carousel control panel, deep in conversation with Tiny Braid Girl. Lily. She's sitting in Jed's chair, with her feet propped up on the table. I check her shoes. Sure enough, they're lime-green Converse.

Jed's leaning over the table facing her, with his back to the carousel.

"The Captain won't be happy," I say.

"He's probably busting heads at the parade." Jaime gets into Captain pose, hands on his hips, and drawls, "Parade's a prime location for hooliganism."

We walk up to the carousel gate and wait while the ride slowly comes to a stop. Jed doesn't bother to open the gate for us, so Jaime unhooks it himself and lets us in. The people who were riding the carousel don't even get off. They just stay on to ride again. There's a mom with a toddler, two twin girls with their dad, and three girls in Arts and Science T-shirts. A wave of worry hits me for a second, because one of them is dark-haired and, from the back, looks a lot like Priya, but when she turns her face, I see that it's not her.

Jaime hops onto the wooden floor of the carousel, and I follow him as he weaves around the animals. I'm trying to guess which is his animal of choice. Probably the dragon or the lion. Maybe the rooster. Something loud.

But he doesn't head to any of these. He walks to the center of the carousel and hovers for a second at the edge of the platform. Then he hops off the platform, grabs the handle of the door that leads to the little hexagon-shaped room, and slips inside.

I've followed him to the edge of the platform, and I stand there, not sure what to do. I look at Jed, who's still got his back to the carousel. The other passengers are all looking at the twin girls, who are viciously fighting over which one of them gets to ride the unicorn. Then I turn back to the door Jaime just vanished into. And I vanish into it, too.

CHAPTER 28

The room is small, about the size of my little bathroom back at home. It's dim and hot and quiet. I feel a little like Pinocchio in the belly of the whale. You can hear the sounds of the outside world—people talking, the parade crowd cheering—but it's all muffled. Softened. It actually reminds me a lot of how I used to feel hiding in the back of the coat closet when I was a kid.

"Is this what you were talking about?" Jaime asks. He's pointing to a big wooden structure, which I realize is the back of the band organ.

I walk over to it slowly, like it's an animal and I don't want to startle it. It's just a little shorter than I am, and it sort of looks like a newspaper press, with a few rolls of paper set up, one on top of the other. I can see the back of the two drums, on either side of the machine, and at the top is the back of a cymbal. On the right side near the floor is a big wheel, which must be what powers the whole thing when it's on—it's in the place where a hand crank would be in a smaller version. It's intricate, and perfect.

"What's the deal with these roll-y things?" Jaime asks, leaning in to take a closer look.

"Those are the music rolls," I explain. "The notches are the different musical notes. It's sort of like . . . you know how the very first computers used punch cards to run? It's kind of like that, like an early computer."

"A really, really early one. Like, for cavemen."

I walk over to the machine. It smells musty in a really comforting way, like a grandma.

"It's exactly like being inside a music box," I say to Jaime. "Right?"

He shrugs. "I never thought of it like that, but . . . yeah, I guess."

He walks over to a section of wall a few feet from the machine and squats to look at something. "Hey, want to see something cool?"

"You mean, cooler than this?"

"To me, yeah," he says, pointing to the wooden beam in the wall. "You need to get close to see it. It's tiny."

I lean over to look at the spot he's pointing at. There's something scratched into the wood — words? No, letters. *J.B.*

"What's that?" I ask.

"My initials."

"Did you . . . did you just do that now?"

"I didn't do it at all," he says. "My dad did."

I'm totally confused now and I must look it, because he explains.

"My initials are all over the park, actually. Vertigo Vortex. The Majestic. The Tree House. The Shooting Star—everywhere."

"But, I mean, why? How?"

Jaime stands up and walks over to the music rolls, so his back is toward me.

"He worked here. My dad, I mean. Pretty much my whole life. On the construction crew. Whenever he built or repaired something, he sneaked in my initials. Both of ours, actually. His name was Javier. So we had the same initials."

Was . . . had. The words linger in the air like a bad smell. They just hover, heavy, so heavy, until finally I can't take it anymore.

"Jaime," I say. I'm nervous because I know he may get mad—really, really mad—but I have to ask. "What happened with your dad?"

He turns to me, and there's this expression on his face—I've never seen anything like it. It's not angry or sad, it's just . . . lost.

It feels like time has stopped in this little box of a room. There's no air, or sound. It's just so still.

And then the whole room explodes. With sound, at least. It's this deafening noise that erupts out of the band organ. It sounds like how a volcano must feel—hot, fast, close. The drums are being beaten right in front of us, and the music rolls are rolling, and the organ is bellowing. Jaime and I both cover our ears, and Jaime runs the few steps to the door, with me right behind him.

But before Jaime can get to the door, it opens on its own. Well, not on its own, exactly. There's a hand pulling the door open, and an arm attached to the hand—a large arm, which is attached to a muscled body wearing a too-tight Foreverland Security shirt.

The Captain.

His wall of a body blocks the little door completely. His lips are moving, but I can't hear what he's saying. I can't hear anything but the thundering of the organ, which is so loud I feel like it's inside my skull. I can't hear what the Captain's saying, but it doesn't matter anyway, because his eyes say it all and what they're saying is: "*It's over.*"

It feels like the little room is shrinking. The sound of the organ is impossibly loud, even with both hands clamped tight over my ears. The Captain's huge body is blocking the only door. There's nowhere to run or hide. It's a standoff with the loudest soundtrack imaginable.

I look at Jaime, who I hope will know what to do. Jaime always has an idea. It's not always the best idea, but it's something.

Not now, though. Now Jaime looks as clueless as I feel, with his hands over his ears, staring straight ahead at the Captain, all deer-in-the-headlights.

"JAIME!" I yell, trying to get his attention. But he can't hear me over the banging of the drums and the cymbal right next to his head. So I grab his elbow, and he looks at me, startled, like he forgot I was here. He looks at me and then he mouths one word.

Fun fact: I can't read lips. So I have no idea what this word is.

"WHAT?" I yell at him. "WHAT?"

But I know he can't hear me, and anyway, it's too late. He's turned his attention back to the Captain. Jaime's reaching into his magical shorts pockets and pulling something out. The walkie-talkie. As soon as the Captain sees it, his face gets bright red, and that vein in his neck starts throbbing like crazy.

Jaime's not a deer in the headlights anymore. He's a bullfighter waving a red cape now, trying to make the Captain mad. Baiting him. Jaime raises the walkie-talkie to his mouth, grinning his whole-face grin right at the Captain, and that's it, that's the final straw. The Captain's moving, running across the tiny room to reach Jaime, with his massive arm outstretched.

I am standing next to Jaime, completely frozen, because what can I do? What can I possibly do? And then Jaime looks right at me, and screams, "GO!" loud enough to break through the wall of noise, and I realize that's what he was mouthing before. *Go.*

That's exactly what I do. As the Captain lunges

for Jaime, I lunge for the door. I grab the handle with my sweating hand and push it open.

I'm abandoning him, I'm thinking as I leap onto the spinning carousel platform.

I'm abandoning him, I'm thinking as my knees bash into the hard metal stirrups of a carousel horse and my stomach crashes into the saddle.

I hear shouts, but I can't tell where they're coming from and there's no time to think or plan or do anything but go, go, go, like Jaime said. I dart around one carousel animal and then another one, and another. I'm dizzy, so dizzy I feel like I might be sick to my stomach, but there is no time for that, either.

I can tell by the music that the carousel is slowing down, but I don't have time to wait for it to come to a stop. I leap off the moving carousel, crashing into the fence that surrounds it, and then I'm running again—dizzy and nauseous and ears ringing from the band organ.

There's no one waiting for the carousel, so I can sprint through the gate and run easily down the path toward who knows where.

"STOP!" I hear a voice call from behind me. "STOP RIGHT WHERE YOU ARE!" It's a man's voice, but I can't stop to see whose it is. I just run faster, pumping my arms, passing an ice cream stand, which is closed, and then the entrance to the Majestic Theater.

The footsteps behind me are getting louder, and I know I'm losing ground, which, honestly, isn't surprising, considering that I run exactly one time a year, for the Fitness-Gram they force us to do in PE. I haven't exactly been training for this high-speed chase, and I can tell that I don't have much more fight in me. So when I get to the end of the Majestic building, instead of running straight, I take a sharp left, swerving to throw the security guard off my scent.

My cool move causes me to lose my balance, and I fall to the ground, landing on my knees. I'm wincing because I feel my knee scab from this morning open up and start to bleed. I'm panting, on all fours, staring at the pavement, thinking that this is it, the end of the line. Because I'm not just staring at the pavement; I'm also staring at a pair of shoes.

Boots, actually.

Black ones.

With safety pins hanging off the laces.

"Door's open," Belle hisses. And then she's yanking me up by the arm and pushing me, hard, toward a red door in the side of the Majestic Theater.

I don't wonder what's behind door number one, mainly because there's no door number two and, also:

Fun fact: Beggars can't be choosers.

I pull on the knob of the door and slip inside.

It's dark on the other side of the door. I grope my way forward and instantly hit a wall, so I guess

I must be standing in some kind of tight space like a hallway. Or a prison cell. I hear voices then, right outside. It's a man's voice, the one that was calling out for me to stop.

"Where'd she go?" he's asking. He sounds out of breath.

"Weird girl? Bad haircut?" Belle replies.

Ouch, I think. *Way to hit a girl when she's down.*

"Yeah," the guy's saying. "Where is she?"

"She just blew through the bushes," Belle says. "Probably going to the parade."

"Thanks," the guy says, but muffled, like he's already taken off.

I lean against the wall then and brace myself for what's coming next. A second later, the door in front of me opens and I hear footsteps—heavy, combat-boot, prepare-for-war steps. Then Belle's voice: "Come on."

I can't see anything, but I follow the sound of her footsteps down the hallway, feeling my way along the wall. I am about as good at this as I am at reading lips. A few steps in and I bash my face into a wall that springs up out of nowhere. I can't help but cry out, because it hurts, and in response, Belle sighs loudly and grabs my elbow to guide me. Her fingers are freakishly cold. It must be from the ice-cold blood running through her veins.

We turn one corner, then another and another until I'm totally disoriented. I'm pretty sure this is exactly what kidnappers do to their captives, to make sure they can never find their way home again. It seems like a bad sign, but what can I do?

I take a mental inventory of the stuff in my backpack, trying to think of something that can be used as a weapon. I am racking my brain for ways to wield hand sanitizer when we make a turn that lands us in a brighter stretch of hallway. The lights aren't on, but there's a red glow coming from somewhere.

Hellfire, is my first thought.

Then I realize it's coming from an exit sign at the end of the hallway.

Belle stops walking. There are two doors in front of us. One of them has a sign that reads PROP ROOM. The other has a sign that reads DANGER. DO NOT ENTER.

I have a pretty good idea which door we're going through.

CHAPTER 29

It's hot in the Danger chamber. Really hot. It feels like I've entered an inferno.

There's a *click*, and then light floods the room. There's a massive metal contraption behind me. A boiler. So that's why it's so hot.

Belle crosses her arms over her chest and leans back against the door.

"Happy now?"

This throws me for a loop.

"You mean, like, in this room . . . or, ummm, in general?"

Belle blinks in excruciating slow motion. I never knew a blink could be this terrifying.

"I mean," she says in a singsong way, like she's talking to a toddler, "are you satisfied with your handiwork?"

It seems like it's probably a rhetorical question, so I don't say anything. But then she doesn't say anything, either, so I think maybe she's expecting an answer.

"This isn't—I mean, I didn't—"

She holds her hand up in a *"stop"* gesture. "He's

totally screwed now, and it's your fault. You know that, right?"

"Jaime?" I say.

"No, Walt Disney."

"Oh," I say. "You're being sarcastic."

"You're going to have to fix things."

"I'm sorry," I say. "But, I mean, he's just a kid, so they can't—like, he can't go to jail or whatever. He didn't really do anything that bad, right?"

Belle tilts her head at me and narrows her eyes. Every time I think she can't get any scarier, she does.

"He didn't tell you?"

"Tell me what?"

"Here," she says, unzipping the Foreverland hoodie she's wearing. She tosses it to me. "Put this on."

And I do, even though it's approximately four hundred degrees in this boiler room and I already feel like I am suffocating.

"This isn't the first time Jaime's squatted here," Belle says. "The last time, when the Captain called the cops, they warned his grandparents they could lose custody if it happened again. They're really old, his grandparents, and if they can't control him, he can't stay there."

"So where will he go?"

"He'll go to foster care, Einstein. Where else?" she says.

"What about his parents?"

"Did I say I was taking questions?" Belle pulls

off her Foreverland baseball cap and tosses it at me. "You've got to fix this mess you made. Even though his grandparents are old and kinda checked out, they're a helluva lot better than foster care."

She nods at the cap I'm holding.

"So put it on and let's go," she says. "Unless you have any other dumb questions that will cost us precious time?"

I shake my head, then shove the cap on.

"Thank God," she says. "I don't have to look at that haircut anymore."

"I did it myself—" I start to say.

"NOBODY CARES!" Belle bellows. She takes two big steps toward me, and now she's right in my face so I can smell her ash breath. "Listen to me, Margaret. Are you listening?"

"Uh-huh," I grunt.

"You are going to need to pull it together now."

"Uh-huh." This seems like the safest reply.

"I need you to help me spring Jaime and get him past the Captain, out of the park, and back to his grandparents. This needs to happen *now*, before the Captain calls the cops. If we can do that, I think—I *hope*—it'll be okay."

"Uh-huh."

Belle walks to the door and grabs the knob, but she doesn't open it. She turns back to look at me, and her eyes are softer, like she might still be part human.

"Jaime's a good person. He's had a really bad year. If he gets booted from his grandparents', that could turn into a bad forever. So this matters. Do you understand?"

"Yeah," I say, even though I don't, really. All I understand is that Belle knows what to do and she needs my help to do it.

I zip up the hoodie and follow Belle out of the boiler room. I have a brief flicker of worry about scabies, but I'm pretty sure all living creatures that are stupid enough to stumble onto Belle's skin die on contact. Also, I have bigger fish to fry.

Belle doesn't lead me back the way we came. Instead, she heads for the exit sign at the end of the short hallway.

"Just keep up with me," she orders. "And act confident."

We bust through the exit door, and now we're on the opposite side of the Majestic, headed, I'm guessing, toward security. Belle walks really fast, almost as fast as Jaime. You'd think those combat boots would weigh her down, but it's like she's got springs in there.

As we speed-walk, she breaks down the plan. I think she learned her plan making from Jaime, because her plan, like his, only has one step. She's going to create a diversion to lure the Captain out of the booth, and I'm going to sneak in and get Jaime out. It seems like a one-person job—like if the

Captain abandons his post, I'm pretty sure Jaime can take care of the rest. But when I point this out to Belle, she gives me a look that's so withering, I feel myself actually shrinking.

"You do know who we're talking about, right? Jaime? Head as thick as a brick wall? Does incredibly stupid crap? I've tried to convince him to go back home . . . more times than I can even count. He's got a thing about leaving this place."

We're walking through Sky City. The parade must be over, because there are people on the paths now. Lots of kids wearing beaded necklaces and cardboard crowns.

"Why do you think I'll be able to convince him, if you couldn't?" I ask.

"Well, for starters, because you have to. You don't want to deal with me if you mess this up." She glares at me and I shrink a little more. "But also? I don't think it's going to be that hard now that he's been caught. I mean, he can be dumb, but he's still got a brain. At least, I hope he does."

"Belle!" calls a voice. I look down the path ahead of us and see the king and queen of Foreverland, still in costume, waving. They're headed toward us. They're clearly a real couple—he's got his arm slung over her shoulders, and she's got her arm around his waist. It's funny to see the royal couple off duty, with collars unbuttoned and crowns all crooked, eating potato chips.

As they get close, my heart starts to race because I haven't been prepped—I don't even know who I'm supposed to be impersonating or anything, and I am sure I look way too young to be working here.

I turn to Belle. "What am—?"

"Say nothing," she hisses. Which sounds good to me.

"Dude, you missed the parade drama," says the king. I remember Jaime telling me his name was Nicky, and knowing this makes me weirdly excited and happy, like I'm an insider. "There was a manhunt."

"*Girl*hunt," corrects the queen. She has long, straight blonde hair, parted in the middle, wide blue eyes, and almost invisible eyebrows.

"It's pathetic, what passes for excitement in this place," Belle snorts.

"Of course, they didn't find her," says Nicky.

"She's still *at large*," the queen says, her mouth full of chips.

Belle smirks. "The Captain must be chomping at the bit."

"Nah, he's too excited about his big catch," says the queen. "He finally got his white whale."

Nicky gives her a confused look. "The Captain caught a whale?"

She rolls her eyes at him. "Read a book, Nicky. I mean that he caught his Moby Dick. That boy he's been obsessed with catching?"

"Listen, I gotta do something for my dad," Belle

says. "Fill me in later?" She starts walking again, which I know is my cue to follow.

"Cool, cool," says Nicky. I'm just starting to relax and my heart is slowing to a normal speed when he calls after us, "Hey, Belle, what's with the sidekick? You got an intern?"

Belle mouths something to him, which he seems to understand, because he nods and then turns to walk off. I, of course, have no idea what she said. If I'd known I was going to have to read so many lips, I would've taken a tutorial or something.

"What'd you tell him?" I ask.

"That you're a Make-A-Wish kid."

"Was that really necessary?" I say. "I'm totally healthy! I mean, do I look—"

"Have you *seen* your haircut?" Belle laughs and rams her bony shoulder into mine. I'm not sure but I think it's supposed to be a sign of friendship. I seize the moment.

"Belle," I say. "What happened to Jaime's parents?"

She shakes her head, and the safety pins hanging off her earrings jingle. Like bells. I wonder if that's where she got her name. "If he wants you to know, he'll tell you. You get info from me on a need-to-know basis. And what you need to know *now* is: Jaime's got to go straight home. Tell him I'm calling the house tomorrow morning, and he better pick up the phone."

"Okay."

"And give him this," she says, pulling a wad of cash out of her shorts pocket and pressing it into my hand. "For the cab."

We're getting close to the security booth. I can make out Schmidt's head in the front window, but there's no one else with him. Jaime and the Captain must be in one of the back rooms.

Belle stops walking to face me.

"Okay, so you'll go around the right side, behind those bushes. From there, you can see the side door—that leads to the room where Jaime is. Captain calls it his interrogation room. I'm going to the back, and I'll get the Captain to come out that way. As soon as he comes out the back, you have to get Jaime out of the side door. Then get him out of the park. It shouldn't be that hard. The park exit's not far."

I nod and start walking toward the bushes.

"Hey, Margaret?" Belle calls. I turn to her.

"Yeah?"

"You got this."

"Okay," I say. But what I am thinking is that I hate it when people say stuff like that. It's the definition of bad luck.

CHAPTER 30

And I'm back to hiding behind the bushes—just like this morning. Only difference is I'm on the opposite side of the booth. Well, that and now I'm doing a break-out instead of a break-in.

I can't believe that it's only been a few hours since Jaime and I were here getting my backpack. It feels like days.

I can see Schmidt's profile in the front window of the booth. He's looking down at something. From the sound effects, I'm guessing it's that video game he's hooked on. I feel a sudden flash of affection for Schmidt. He's not a bad guy. In fact, he seems really nice. All he wants to do is play his video game and collect bobbleheads and help people find stuff they've lost. He doesn't deserve the way the Captain's always yelling at him.

I'm itching to write a *SCHMIDT* acrostic, but before I can even consider it, my downtime's over. Belle's walked over to the front window and is saying something to Schmidt that I can't make out. He hands his phone to her, and she jabs and swipes on it until the high-pitched sound effects turn into a loud *doo-doo-doo-DOO* victory tune.

Is she playing a video game? Now? After she rushed me over here like Jaime's life was on the line?

Just as I'm starting to think that she's totally lost it, she slides the phone back to Schmidt and walks around the booth toward the back door. Schmidt's on his feet, looking at his phone with this expression of unbelieving joy, like he just won the lottery.

I realize this was part of Belle's plan—now that he's moved into what is obviously a super-cool level, Schmidt is absolutely fixated on the game. The whole security booth could fall down around him, and he wouldn't so much as look up.

It does not surprise me that Belle is a master gamer. She is the kind of person who can do anything—especially if it involves annihilation.

Like she's reading my mind, Belle unleashes some serious destruction on the back door of the booth. She's pounding on it with both fists, yelling "CAPTAIN!" until the door opens a crack and I see the Captain's head peek out.

I can't hear much of what they're saying, but he shakes his head and starts to disappear again. This makes Belle raise her voice.

"So is that what you want me to tell my father?" she yells. With her hands on her hips, she looks like a five-foot-tall punk warrior.

The Captain opens the door all the way then and walks out. He crosses his huge arms over his chest and leans back against the door. Even from here, I can see the telltale vein in his neck throbbing. The guy would have no chance against a lie detector test. That vein would give him away.

"Talk," he growls at Belle.

This is my cue. I squeeze through the bushes, holding my backpack in front of me this time so it won't get caught. I walk quickly to the side entrance, thinking *confident confident confident.*

I hear Belle's voice from around the corner, threatening him with terms like *legal action* and *deal breaker.* She's trying to make him mad, and it is working.

"I'm busy right now," the Captain spits out. You can hear his teeth gritting so hard, he can barely get the words out. "How 'bout we discuss this later?"

"Maybe we need to get my father on the phone," she's spitting right back. "Settle this once and for all."

I'm fifteen feet from the side door, then ten, then five, and then my hand is on the doorknob, turning. Or trying to turn. It's not budging. It's locked.

Now what?

I can't knock on the door. The Captain will hear. And I'm not exactly an expert lock picker.

Then I have an idea. I grab my notebook out of

my backpack, quietly tear a piece of paper out, and scribble:

Oh hi.

Perhaps you'd like to

Exit

Now.

I don't know if Jaime will get it. I don't know if he'll actually get the paper, and I also don't know if he'll understand it even if he does. But it's all I can think to do. Within five seconds I'm sliding the paper under the door. Then I wait.

Meanwhile, the fight between the Captain and Belle is heating up.

"Listen—" she's saying.

"No, *you* listen to *me*."

I stare at the doorknob so hard, I feel like I might melt the metal with my eyes. Belle is now full-on shouting at the Captain, and I'm worried this is going to attract a lot of attention to the booth, where I am just waiting, completely exposed, in the middle of a jailbreak. I stare at the doorknob and tell myself I'll wait five more seconds before I run back to the bushes.

Five
Four
Three

I hear a whole bunch of stuff then, all at the same time:

1. Yelling from the other side of the door.
2. An enormous clatter.
3. The door in front of me opening, and then slamming shut.

And in the middle of all that noise, there's Jaime, standing right in front of me.

"Took you long enough," he says. He's grinning, that superstrength grin that is totally the wrong reaction right now but also kind of the perfect reaction, too. A very Jaime reaction.

I am so relieved to see him that for a second I think I'm going to hug him or something disastrous like that. Instead, I punch him in the arm and say, "You *could* say thanks."

"Thanks," he says. "Better late than never."

Then he nods his head, and I must be catching on to Jaime-ese, because I know he means "*Let's go.*" When he takes off running toward the front of the booth, in the direction of the park gates, I'm right next to him. We make it only a few feet, though, before the Captain appears directly in front of us.

CHAPTER 31

The Captain freezes. So does Jaime. Their eyes are locked. They remind me of cowboys in a stand-off, hands on their holsters, waiting to see who'll draw first.

It's Jaime. He does an about-face, yanking me forward by the hand. Then we run.

Fun fact: I can't outrun a toddler, much less the captain of security.

Contradictory fact: I am, somehow, doing it.

I pump my arms and pound the pavement so hard, I almost expect the ground to give under my feet. My legs have hijacked my body and are totally running the show, while my mind just watches, unbelieving. There is no sound but my own breath and this white noise like a waterfall, which must be my blood pumping in my head.

My body has found a rhythm that makes sense, and I am soaring over the ground. My feet are cata-pulting me forward so fast, I feel like a panther or a puma—one of those big cats that cars and sneakers are named after.

I can hear footsteps behind me, and I can tell the

Captain's close, but I don't feel worried. I don't feel anything, actually. I don't think anything, either. There is nothing but the coolness of the night air hitting my face and the steady pounding of my feet and the squeezing of Jaime's hand around mine.

We run through Tot Town down empty paths, past Baby Hells Angels and the spinning teacups, and then Jaime makes a right turn down this little path that has a dead-end feel to it. There are no rides, no concession stands, not even any benches. Nothing looks familiar here.

"Getting tired?" barks the Captain's voice from behind me. It's close, much closer than seems safe. And as soon as he asks the question, I *am* tired. I am suddenly incredibly tired. Except that *tired* is the wrong word for it. I'm suddenly out of fuel, an empty gas tank. I feel like my legs are going to collapse.

And that's when I realize that we're running directly toward a chain-link fence. A fence with a gate that's locked with a padlocked chain. The fence surrounds what looks like a junkyard. I am sure Jaime's going to turn, but instead he picks up speed, pulling me toward the fence.

I'm panting much too hard to speak, but I am praying that Jaime does not screw everything up. I am praying that what looks like a terrible idea is actually a great idea for reasons I don't know.

Jaime lets go of my hand and lunges for the gate.

He pries the two gates apart, and there's enough slack in the chain for his skinny body to slip through.

"Gimme your backpack!" he's yelling, still holding the gate open. I fling it at his outstretched hand, and then I'm at the gate, turning my head sideways so it will fit through the gap that Jaime's made.

My head is through and then my top half, too, but before I can pull my right leg through, there is a tug on my foot. It's the Captain scrambling to get ahold of me.

Jaime yanks on my arm on one side of the fence while the Captain yanks on my foot on the other. I feel like a wishbone. For a split second, I worry I'm going to crack in two. Then the Captain pulls down hard on my heel while I pull up hard on my leg. I feel something give, but it's not my body, it's my sandal. My shoe flies off, and the rest of me slips through the gate.

The Captain flies backward, falling hard on his back, clutching my shoe.

"Looking for Cinderella?" Jaime asks with a massive smirk.

Before Jaime can have a good laugh, the Captain roars a barbaric war cry and leaps through the air, hurling himself at the fence. When he makes contact, his feet are already at the level of our waists. Then, like a ninja, he starts climbing up the fence, grunting.

Fun fact: Metallica calisthenics work wonders.

"C'mon!" Jaime's yelling, and then we're running through this no-man's-land. It must be some kind of maintenance area, a workshop, because there are all kinds of ride parts here, lying on the asphalt. There are some Shooting Star cars with their lap bars stuck at weird angles, a bunch of carousel animals lying on tarps, half-painted. There is an entire Pirate's Cove ship covered in graffiti, with pieces falling off of it. There's even a chunk of the Tot Town Tree House—one of the towers, with a huge dent in the roof. I walk quickly around the stuff, feeling totally unbalanced because I'm only wearing one shoe.

A rattling sound makes me look over at the fence, and, wow, the Captain must have some serious training, because he's already over the top and jumping down into the lot. I'm standing next to the Pirate's Cove ship, so I scramble up the short rope ladder onto the wooden deck.

Jaime doesn't follow me. Instead, he runs into the Tree House tower and climbs the spiral stairs inside. He stops at one of the highest windows to lean out and yell, "Run run run, as fast as you can, you can't catch me—"

"Wanna bet?" the Captain yells. He's running into the Tree House tower now, and as he rushes up the stairs, Jaime climbs out the window, pulling himself up onto the dented roof.

The tower's not attached to anything on the ground, and all the running and climbing is making it shake. I'm sure that the tower's going to topple over, and if it does, it's taking the Captain and Jaime with it.

The Captain must realize this, too, because he's leaning out the window Jaime just climbed out of and yelling up at him, "Get down before you get us both killed."

Jaime puts both hands on his hips and peers down at the Captain.

"Down?" Jaime says. "Sure."

I know he's going to jump before he does it. I know it, and I want to stop him, but before I can form the scream in my throat, he's already airborne.

Jaime doesn't just jump off the roof. He dives off. He dives headfirst, and then he's somersaulting, his knees bent all the way to his chest, his arms around his knees. I have this instinct to catch him, but this, I know, would be a terrible idea. So I just step back and close my eyes so I don't have to see his head hit the wooden floor I'm standing on.

There's a loud thud and also a scream. I realize after a second that the scream is coming from my mouth.

Then someone's shaking me and I open my eyes, bracing myself for something gruesome. But it's Jaime shaking me and his head—his thick head—is in one piece.

"I always land on my feet," he says in this "duh"

kind of way, but I can't argue with him, because the Captain is already climbing up the ship's rope ladder.

I'm afraid the Captain's going to grab me because he's close, really close, but he ignores me completely. It's like I'm not even there. He's got his eyes glued to Jaime, who's leaping around the ship almost like he's dancing. He's jumping from one bench to the next. He's swinging around the pole in the middle of the ship. Every time the Captain corners him, Jaime dodges him, until he ends up on the far side of the ship where the gangplank is—the fore? the aft? I still don't know what you call it. It's narrow there, and there's no way for Jaime to get past without the Captain grabbing him. Jaime backs up in small steps until he's right against the plank. And then he steps on.

"Jaime!" I yell out. The Captain doesn't even turn around. He's stepped onto the plank, too, and he's walking closer and closer to Jaime, who keeps backing away.

There's a sound at the fence. When I turn, I see Schmidt and Scarecrow Security Guy unlocking the padlocked gate. They fling the gate open and run through—Scarecrow Guy first and Schmidt huffing and puffing behind him.

"Go!" Jaime is yelling at me. "Go!"

But this time, I don't go. I'm not leaving Jaime.

"Stop!" I yell at the Captain's back. He doesn't

turn around. I wonder for a second if he can even hear me. Maybe I'm so invisible, I have no voice. I try again, louder this time.

"LEAVE HIM ALONE!" I scream. I know I'm making sound because my throat hurts from the effort. But it's like I'm not there. The Captain doesn't so much as twitch in my direction.

I should be able to do something, I think. *I want to be able to do something.*

Jaime's almost at the end of the plank now. It wouldn't be hard for him to jump down—it's not that high, only about five feet, but he can't, because standing on the ground below are Schmidt and Scarecrow Guy. Jaime can't get down, and he can't get past the Captain. He's stuck.

But I'm not.

I take a step forward and stumble over something. It's a wooden sword, splintered, its paint peeling off. It must have fallen off the mast beside me, where its identical twin is mounted. I land hard on my already-scraped knee. I feel the fresh scabs open up and a warm wetness on my kneecap. I don't know if it's the pain or something else, but suddenly I'm reaching for the wooden sword and picking it up. It's heavier than it looks, so I need both hands to lift it.

Then I'm moving fast, toward the Captain. He's halfway across the plank, reaching for Jaime, who's at the very end. I have no idea what I'm doing. It's like it's not even me doing it. I run to the plank, then step on it.

I lift the heavy sword up with both hands and I swing it at the Captain, hitting him on the side of his left arm.

"What the—" he yells.

He spins around to look at me, but as he turns, he loses his balance and then he's tilting wildly to the side, his arms windmilling and his legs kicking out fast. It kind of looks like he's tap-dancing in the air, except that the expression on his face is like something from a horror movie—a combination of shock and fear.

I step back off the plank and drop the wooden sword to the floor, where it makes a huge clatter that's not nearly loud enough to cover the sound of the Captain hitting the ground.

Now Schmidt and Scarecrow Guy are rushing over to the Captain, and Jaime is sprinting down the plank to me. We shimmy down the rope ladder of the ship and run toward the open gate.

CHAPTER 32

The Captain's howling, and Schmidt and Scarecrow Guy are yelling, too, and Jaime's saying something as we run, but I can't hear any of their words over the cataclysmic thunderstorm of fear and confusion in my head.

What did I do? What did I do?

"C'mon," Jaime's yelling. I try to hurry, but it's hard to run fast wearing just one sandal. We're still only halfway to the gate when I hear the Captain's voice yelling, "GO GO GO! GET THEM!"

I make the mistake of looking behind me then and see Schmidt and Scarecrow Guy getting to their feet and running after us.

Jaime takes us through the gate, and then he makes a left turn, racing through a really dimly lit area toward a big tree. On one side of the tree is a security cart, and on the other side is a blue pickup truck with a blue tarp covering the back. I can see the top of a folded-up ladder poking out of the tarp.

"Get under the tarp," Jaime says. He gets down on one knee, and it looks like he's asking me to marry him, which is confusing, until I realize he's

224

letting me use his knee as a step stool so I can hoist myself over the side of the truck. I climb in, fast and clumsy, and land on a bunch of paint cans, making way too much noise. I crawl under the tarp, next to the ladder because there's more space under there for my head. There's all sorts of stuff in here—boxes and cords and ropes. It must be a maintenance truck.

"Just keep still," Jaime says, climbing in behind me. "I don't think they saw us get in."

It takes me a minute to find his face because it's dark under the tarp, but once my eyes get adjusted, I can make out the whites of his eyes next to me, on the other side of the ladder. The little I can see is tinted blue from the tarp. It kind of feels like we're at the bottom of the ocean. I don't know whether it's this or the old familiar feeling of hiding on top of paint cans, but I feel more relaxed.

"Are you okay?" Jaime whispers.

"I don't know," I whisper back. "I mean. I guess."

"What'd you do?"

"I—I don't know. I didn't mean to. He just, he fell . . . I think he got hurt." There's this huge lump in my throat, so big it feels like I'm choking on it. "I'm a terrible person."

"I hope not," Jaime whispers. "Because if you're a terrible person, then what am I?"

The sound of footsteps gets louder.

"I don't see them," comes Scarecrow Guy's voice.

"Captain, you should go to Medical," Schmidt's saying. "They should look at your hand. It could be broken."

"It's nothin' but a sprain," the Captain snarls. "And I don't want to lose 'em. They've got to be close by."

"We've got a better chance of finding them in the cart," says Scarecrow Guy. "We can look on our way to Medical."

Their voices are close now, and my heart speeds up. I'm breathing so hard, I feel like they must be able to hear it.

"Fine," the Captain barks. "But Schmidt, I want you to stay here. I know that kid. He's hidin', like the little rat he is. But he can't stay hidden long. Her, too. I want the girl, too."

Jaime's eyes find mine in the dark.

"Yessir! I got it, sir! I will secure the parameter," Schmidt says.

"The perimeter, Schmidt. Perimeter."

"Of course, sir. Of course. I'll check the bathrooms right now."

I hear the hum of the security cart next to us starting up, and then it drives off. There's the sound of footsteps getting softer. I guess Schmidt's walking to the bathrooms.

"What now?" I whisper.

"We hang tight."

"But the park's closing soon. And you need to get out."

"Yeah, I know."

"So maybe we should just run."

He shakes his head. "Too risky. It's really far to the front gates, and the park's pretty empty now. They'll spot us in a second."

"So, what—?"

"Shhhh! Someone's coming."

He's right. A girl's voice is getting louder, like she's walking toward us.

"I don't *know* where I am, Mom. If I knew, I wouldn't be lost."

The voice is familiar.

Which is impossible.

Still, it is.

"Okay, I'm sorry. I know it's not your fault . . . No, Mom, I'm not. I'm not having any asthma . . . I'll probably start, though, if you don't stop stressing me out."

"Oh my God," I say out loud. Because I cannot believe it.

Fun fact: "It's a small world" isn't just a ride in Disneyland.

Jaime's mouthing something at me and this time, I get it: *Who is it?*

Priya, I mouth back.

He shakes his head and makes a "*huh*?" expression.

"Priya," I whisper. "My best friend? Ex–best friend?"

Priya's voice is getting closer.

"I don't know—Sky City, maybe? There's nothing around here. I can't really tell."

"Call her over!" Jaime's saying.

"What? No!"

"She can help us get out."

"No. No way. That's a terrible—"

But he's already lifting up the tarp and whispering, "Priya! Over here!"

I push him back under the tarp and glare at him. Then I hear Priya say, "Mom, let me call you right back. In, like, two secs."

I know Priya will come over, even though she shouldn't. I mean, it's the dead of night in a dim, deserted area, and a stranger hiding in the back of a pickup truck just called her over. Nobody in their right mind would come over. But I know Priya, and I know she cannot resist the temptation of a major drama, even if that drama might possibly involve her getting ax murdered. It's why I loved being her best friend. She always brought the fun.

I peek out from under the tarp, and sure enough, Priya's walking over. I don't think she can see me, because I'm hidden in the shadow of the tarp, but I can see her. She looks a lot taller and thinner. She's wearing these cutoff denim shorts that we used to make fun of girls for wearing. I bet she had a fight with her mother about those. Her Arts and Science T-shirt is tied in a knot on the side of her waist, and she's got on a pair of big hoop earrings. She's wearing a zebra-stripe backpack, so I guess her family found it after all.

Even though she looks really different, the way she walks, with her shoulders flung back and her chin raised, like she's not taking any prisoners—that's exactly the same. She fishes something out of her backpack and holds it in front of her as she takes small, careful steps toward the truck.

"I have pepper spray," Priya is announcing, "and I'm not afraid to use it."

I can't help but smile. It's pure Priya.

"Shhhh!" Jaime hisses at her. "Just stand nearby and pretend you're talking on your phone, and we'll explain."

"We?" she shoots back, but in a whisper.

"Me and Margaret."

Priya breaks into a run then, holding the pepper spray in front of her. She yanks the tarp up.

"Margaret? Oh my God, Margaret, are you okay?"

"She's fine," Jaime says, but Priya whips around and holds the pepper spray at his eye level, with her finger over the nozzle.

"I didn't ask you," she spits out. Then, without taking her eyes off Jaime, she asks, "Margaret, who is this guy? What's going on?"

"It's fine, Priya," I say. "He's a friend. He's help-ing me."

"Helping you how?" she asks, with her finger still on the nozzle.

"Helping me not get caught by security, actually. So it'd be great if you could . . . uh . . . be quiet and, you know, put the tarp down and stuff."

She lowers the pepper spray and looks at me. "Seriously?"

"Seriously. Can you make it look like you're talking on your phone? In case someone passes by?"

She squints at me. "Are you sure you're okay?"

"Positive," I tell her.

"Did you—oh my God, when did you cut your hair? And bangs?" She squeals with excitement. "You've always wanted bangs! They look amazing!"

"I did it myself, actually"

"Get out. You did not!" Priya's eyes are wide. "Seriously, I love it. It's like, perfect for your face—"

"Could we do the hair talk later?" Jaime chimes in. "When we're not in hiding?"

Priya lets the tarp fall down over us and steps back.

"I don't know about this guy, Margaret," she says. "He seems obnoxious."

"I'm right here," Jaime says.

"I'm aware," she shoots back.

Her phone starts ringing then, and she pulls it out of her pocket and puts it to her ear.

"Hi, Mom. Yeah, I think I know where to go now . . . as soon as I can . . . yeah, I have my pepper spray . . . I know . . . I know . . . I *know*."

She ends the call but keeps the phone at her ear, like I asked her to.

"Nobody's even around here, you know," she says.

"Yeah, but there's a security guy right over there," says Jaime, "and he's coming back any second. So can we—?"

"Margaret, your parents are *freaking out*," Priya says. "They called everyone. They are really worried. So was I! I was up till three last night. Do you see these bags under my eyes? All you. I almost didn't come today."

"I'm sorry."

"It's okay. It actually . . . it made me think. We should talk. Like, not *now* obviously."

"Yeah, not now," Jaime pipes up.

"Nobody's talking to you, tough guy," Priya says. "I just . . . I miss you, Margaret. I really do."

This is exactly what I've been hoping would happen for an entire year. It's crazy that this reunion is happening here, now, with me hiding under a tarp, but it still makes me really happy and relieved.

"I miss you, too," I say. "And I'm coming home. Right now, in fact. I can ride back with you. But the thing is, we need to get Jaime out of here first."

"So he's not really helping you. You're helping him."

"We're helping each other. He really needs to get out of here without being seen."

"And you want me to do what? Loan him my cloak of invisibility? Drat, I left it at home."

Jaime asks, "Can you drive this thing? I think the keys are in the ignition."

She doesn't say anything.

"So," Jaime says. "Can you?"

"Oh, you're serious? Umm, no. I cannot drive a *pickup truck*."

"C'mon, it's not hard. You just—"

"Shhhh!" Priya's hissing. "Someone's coming."

"Young lady? Young lady! You really shouldn't be here."

It's Schmidt. I can tell he's been walking fast because he's out of breath. "The park's about to close. You need to make your way to the front gates."

"That's what I'm trying to do," Priya says. "Except I'm totally lost."

"Yes, well, the gates are on the other side of the park. You'll have to walk down this path, then make a right when you see the frozen lemonade stand—"

Priya's phone rings again. When she picks up, her mom is shouting so loud, I can hear her from where I'm sitting.

"Mom . . . Mom, stop flipping out. I'm with

232

a security guard . . . He's going to drive me to the front gates." Then, to Schmidt, "Right?"

"Well, I don't know about that, young lady," he says. "I have responsibilities —"

"My mom wants to talk to you." She must be handing him the phone, because Schmidt is saying, "Hello, Steven Schmidt here . . . uh-huh . . . yes, ma'am, I understand . . . of course . . . no, I don't have a daughter . . . yes, but I can't just abandon my . . . no, no, no, that's not necessary . . . ma'am, please, just calm . . . yes . . . yes . . . yes . . . all right."

There's a pause, and then Priya asks, "So . . . ?"

"Let's go," says Schmidt. The truck shakes as they step inside. Once he turns it on, it begins to vibrate.

"Your mother is a very frightening woman," says Schmidt.

"Tell me about it," says Priya.

CHAPTER 33

Schmidt is a terrible driver. He swerves and stops short and speeds up unexpectedly. It's a disaster for us in the back, because there are all sorts of tools and equipment that are sliding all over the place, hitting us. The ladder is tied down, so we hold on to that, which helps.

The windows in the front are open and I can hear Priya asking Schmidt if he's allowed to use Tasers.

"Your friend is a nightmare," Jaime whispers.

I smile. "I'm pretty sure she thinks the same thing about you."

"Seems like your parents were worried. They'll be glad to have you home."

"Yeah." I look over at Jaime, whose eyes suddenly look droopy, like he's gotten really, really tired. And sad. He looks so sad.

I know we only have a few minutes before we get to the gates, and once we do, he needs to get through them immediately. We don't have much time left. And I have to know.

"Jaime," I whisper. "Why'd you come here? What happened to your parents?"

He drops his head and is quiet for a few seconds. I hear Schmidt in the front seat, telling Priya about the weirdest lost items he's ever had in the Lost and Found. I hear something about a can opener.

When Jaime looks back up at me, his eyes are bright.

"It was just my dad and me," he finally says. "I never had a mom. Or I did, I guess, but she took off when I was a baby, and I haven't heard from her since."

My stomach clenches up. This is so much worse than I was expecting.

"Jaime," I whisper. "I mean, I'm—that's . . . awful."

Jaime shrugs. "Sure, I guess, but not really. My dad always said she wasn't cut out to be a mom. I think it's probably better that she left before I could remember her. I don't miss her. I wonder about her, but I don't miss her." Jaime looks down at his hands and says, "She's not the one I miss."

He looks like he has more to say but he can't bring himself to say it. He looks so small suddenly—and delicate, too. I can't help reaching out and grabbing his hand in mine. Then he looks at me, his dark eyes glowing in the blue light.

"My dad died," he says. "One year and twelve days ago. It was—" He clears his throat. "It was a construction accident. He did subcontractor jobs on the side for extra cash. He was on the roof of some guy's house, and he, um, he fell."

I want him to know I'm listening, that I'm right here, but I don't have any idea what I could possibly say. So I just squeeze his hand tight.

"He was a great dad, you know? I mean, he wasn't perfect. Nobody's perfect, but he was funny and a good cook and he made me feel like I was . . . so special. Like he'd won the jackpot by getting me as his son. Which doesn't make any sense, because all I do is mess up. I don't think and I go too far and I'm always in trouble. But still, he acted like he was so, so lucky to be my dad, like I was a prize."

I nod, not daring to say a word. I'm afraid if I do, he'll stop talking.

"When he died, my mom's parents moved here from Puerto Rico to take care of me. And my grandparents, they're nice or whatever, but they're strangers. The first time I met them was at my dad's funeral. They're not my family. *He* was my family. This was our home."

When he looks back at me, his face is wet. The tears in his eyes make them shine like lanterns.

"He loved this place. He was so proud to work here—to make it special, and safe. The Shooting Star was his favorite. I was one of the first people to ever ride it, you know, with him."

"Wow," I say.

Jaime sighs softly. "I know it's kind of a

rinky-dink park compared to the others, but to him, it was the best amusement park in the world. To him, it really was magic. And now, I guess—well, I want it to be true, the Foreverland motto."

"You want the magic to never end," I say. It's exactly why I came here, too.

He nods, fast. Then he pulls his hand away from mine and uses his palm to wipe his wet face.

"I wish . . ." I say. "I wish there was something I could do."

"There is." He sniffs and then sits up straighter, getting excited. "You can go home and make it count. You're not some nobody, Margaret. You're the girl that spent the night in a Haunted House and gave herself a hard-core haircut and fought the captain of security. You're the girl who freed me."

I am crying now, for so many reasons. I'm crying for Jaime, boy wonder, orphan. I'm crying because he has no parents while I have all of mine—dumb parents, sure, but still, a mother and a father who can't sleep if I'm not there. And suddenly, I miss them so much. I miss the family we used to be, which I know is gone for good. But I also miss *them*, too, separate, apart. Suddenly, I am so homesick. I'm the click-my-heels-three-times-and-think-of-home kind of homesick. I want to see my dad's toothy grin and smell my mother's orange perfume, and I want to show Gwen all the acrostics

I've written. I want to walk through the door of my house even if that red suitcase is still there. Which, I know, it will be.

I'm crying because I can't bear to go back home and I can't bear not to. I'm crying because I don't want to get any older or for things to get even more complicated, but also I can't wait. And I'm crying, maybe most of all, because I know that any minute, we will pull up to the front gates and Jaime will vanish into the night, as mysteriously as he appeared yesterday. I know this is goodbye.

"It'll be okay," Jaime is whispering.

I sniffle. "I should be telling you that."

"Well, what can I say? You're a slacker. I always have to do the heavy lifting."

I roll my eyes and then dry them with the sleeve of my hoodie.

The truck makes a wide turn and starts slowing.

"We're almost there," Schmidt says loudly.

"Thanks," Priya says.

"I'll pull right up to the gates," he almost shouts. "So any passengers on board can exit quickly."

Jaime and I look at each other.

"He knows?" I whisper.

Jaime shrugs. "Life is full of surprises."

"And some of them are even good surprises," I say. "The ratio might be better than fifty-fifty. Could be as high as sixty-forty."

"Steven Schmidt," I hear Priya say. "You're a good guy. You know that?"

"Thank you," Schmidt says. "Thanks very much."

"I see my mom," Priya says.

"I *hear* your mom," he replies.

I want to ask Jaime if he'll be okay, but I know he'll just crack a joke, so instead I pull the wad of cash out of my pocket and hand it to him.

"Belle wanted you to have this, for a cab. She said she's calling your house in the morning and you'd better pick up the phone."

He sticks the money in his pocket and shakes his head. "No faith in me at all."

I suddenly feel this desperate need to give him something, too. I unzip my backpack and pull Darling out. Then I press her into Jaime's hands.

"Really?" His eyebrows are raised. "I thought you never leave a bunny behind."

"I'm not leaving her," I say. "I'm setting her free."

He looks down at Darling, and the corners of his mouth turn up in a quiet smile. Then he squeezes her body into his bottomless shorts pocket, so that only her floppy head sticks out.

"Plus," I say, "she'll keep an eye on you. Make sure you're okay."

"I will be," he says with a nod, and then his face turns serious. "I came here because I thought my dad was still here, in the rides he built, in the initials he carved. And he is."

The truck is slowing to a stop.

"But he's not just here, you know? This isn't the only place I can find him."

My heart is pounding now because there is so much I want to tell him and no time to say any of it.

"Jaime!" I blurt. ". . . Thanks."

"For what?"

"For saving my life."

"Do me a favor. Stay away from hot dogs, okay?"

"I didn't mean just that."

"Well, in that case, thank you, too. For the same thing."

I can hear Priya's mom shouting, "Ten years! That's how much you took off my life! Wandering around in the dark by yourself! And you, what kind of a security person has to be convinced to escort a young girl to the exit? You should be ashamed of yourself!"

"I am, ma'am," Schmidt says. "I am ashamed."

Jaime peeks out from under the tarp on his side.

"All clear," Jaime says. "I better take off."

"Okay."

"Hey, Margarita?"

"Yeah?"

"Check your notebook."

Then a bright light pours into our hiding spot as he lifts up the tarp and climbs over the side. Up he goes, and then the tarp falls back down and I am alone.

My notebook.

Check my notebook.

My heart is pounding as I pull my notebook out and open the front cover. The first page has been folded into an arrow shape. I unfold it quickly, my hands trembling. I'm nervous and excited, like I've discovered a treasure map.

There, in Jaime's terrible chicken-scratch scrawl, is an acrostic.

An acrostic of my name.

He's used the spine of the acrostic that I wrote on the train ride over, but he's filled in the rest.

Maybe one day you'll

Admit I'm

Right. You've got more

Guts than

Anyone. If you believe it, you'll be

Ready. You'll be ready for

Every

Thing.

I read the acrostic again, and again, and then another time. Every time I read it, I feel less sad, less scared, and more excited.

If you believe it, you'll be ready.
If you believe.

I slam the notebook closed, toss it in my back-pack, and lift up the tarp. Then I climb out of the truck and walk over to Priya and her family. Schmidt's gone, but Mrs. Kumari is still giving Priya a piece of her mind. When she sees me, she stops midsentence and stares.

"Hi, Mrs. Kumari," I say. "You got new glasses. They look great."

"Margaret?" Mrs. Kumari asks, like she can't believe her eyes.

"Told you," Zara chimes in, her arms folded across her chest.

"Margaret!" Mrs. Kumari says. "Where have you been? What are you doing here? Why are you only wearing one shoe?"

"I'm really sorry I worried you guys. Can I get a ride home with you?"

She looks at Mr. Kumari and then back at me.

"Of course," she says, blinking.

"Thanks." I slip off my one sandal, shove it in my backpack, and toss the bag at Priya. "Can you wait just a minute? There's something I've got to do."

"But you're not wearing any shoes! What—" Mrs. Kumari starts to say, but I hear Priya telling her that she's going to explain everything. Their voices get softer as I turn my back to them and run into Sky City. The ground is cool under my bare feet.

The park is closing any minute, but it's not closed yet. If I hurry, I can still make it onto the Shooting Star. It's the last ride of the night, and the first for me.

ACKNOWLEDGMENTS

This roller coaster ride would not have been possible without the luminous Erin Stein, and her prodigious patience, instinct, and vision. A huge thanks is owed to the whole Imprint team supreme, masterful and also, delightful, including John Morgan, Nicole Otto, and Weslie Turner. To Michael Bourret, I offer heaps of gratitude, as much for his honesty and acumen as for his faith and encouragement, which is renewing.

Many thanks to the incredibly talented and generous authors Gitty Daneshvari, Matthew Swanson, Suzanne Selfors, Nicole Panteleakos, Courtney Sheinmel, and Kathleen Lane, for their support and kindness. Thanks to Kimberly McCreight, for her indispensable counsel in things literary and beyond. Special thanks to Miranda Beverly-Whittemore, the kind of writer and friend who will not only drop everything to spend a morning brainstorming titles, but do it gladly. To my early readers: Annie Smith as well as Liam and Emma Harty, thank you for your fantastically constructive feedback. Thank you to my forever-little sisters, Melissa and Courtney, my sister-like cousins, Alanna and Sidney, and my Zia Franca, whose extra-deep closets were always the best for hiding. *Grazie mille* to my grandmother Verusca Cavaricci, for too many things to begin to name, and to my father, Dr. Nicholas Caccavo, and mother, the original Margaret.

The thanks owed to my husband, David Kear, is massive and knows no bounds. His keen editorial eye saved this book more than once. His love saved me too many times to count.

To Stella, my high-flying, thrill-seeking, brave-hearted girl, thank you for teaching me to love flight and velocity. To Valentina, my marveler, thank you for making me believe in a magic that never ends. Here's to gutsy girls who never feel invisible. Here's to joyrides.

Last, but really first, I offer gratitude to Giovanni Kear. In a special way, this book owes its life to him. One sunny afternoon, my son and I went walking through the streets of Brooklyn, as we are wont to do. On this day, though, we dreamed up a book together. Over the course of seven city blocks, the entire skeleton of this book, and its heart, were formed. Second star to the right, my boy, and straight on till morning.